Simon says

urbanepublications.com

First published in Great Britain in 2016 by Urbane Publications Ltd
Suite 3, Brown Europe House, 33/34 Gleamingwood Drive, Chatham, Kent ME5 8RZ

A CIP catalogue record for this book is available from the British Library.

ISBN 978-1-910692-48-6
MOBI 978-1-910692-50-9
EPUB 978-1-910692-49-3

Design and Typeset by Julie Martin
Cover by Julie Martin
Printed and bound by CPI Group (UK) Ltd, Croydon, CR0 4YY

urbanepublications.com

The publisher supports the Forest Stewardship Council® (FSC®), the leading international forest-certification organisation.
This book is made from acid-free paper from an FSC®-certified provider. FSC is the only
forest-certification scheme supported by the leading environmental organisations, including Greenpeace.

This book is dedicated to my wife Zoe and our children - Jasmine, Joe and Natty.

Acknowledgements...

I would like to start by acknowledging the influence of films on the writing of this novel; particularly romantic comedies – from "Bringing Up Baby" to "Four Weddings and a Funeral". I believe the skill of romance and comedy working together is undervalued and my thanks go to the cinematic greats I grew up watching.

My family and friends continue to support and help me in so many ways and I would like to thank them all.

I would like to acknowledge a very special thank you to my dear friend, more like a brother to me, Shane Garrigan. He has been, and continues to be, the Sundance Kid to my Butch Cassidy (although I'm certainly not comparing myself to the incredible Paul Newman!).

I would like to add a special thanks to Guy Mankowski for his ongoing support and encouragement.

My wife and children are my life support – an endless source of enthusiasm, happiness, motivation and energy. I wouldn't have written this book without them and the main theme of love is for them.

Finally I want to say a massive thanks to Matthew Smith, founder and MD of Urbane Publications. Matthew renewed my belief in the excitement and value of being published. His energy, honesty, collaboration and drive have made me feel the thrill of books again – which, after twenty years as a bookseller, and a lot of disappointments, is akin to a miracle.

Thank you!

Chapter ONE...

Simon Templar had to balloon his mouth to fairly comic proportions to contain the swig of lime soda. His cheeks were so stretched in incredulity and the immediacy of shock (to the point where the skin around his lips felt as if it would split and that he might spray the entire bar) after his very drunk and soon-to-be father-in-law said the following words:

'You know what, Simon, you really *are* a saint. I mean, I love my daughter and I'd forgive her anything. But I think it was incredibly tolerant of you to let her go out with you *and* that Dean bloke when you first got together. For *six* whole months too. And just so that she could have her pick of the best. So glad she chose you. He was a real creep; hands all over her all the sodding time. Cheers to you, Saint.'

They both, usually, laughed at the reference to the television programme, although Simon *had* heard the same joke/reference throughout his life and he thought he was ready to physically assault the next person who nodded and winked and made comments along the lines that he neither looked like Roger Moore or the later *Saint* incarnation Ian Ogilvy. The name had been his father's idea – with the surname Templar in place already, and the series being such a hit, who could resist? Moore played the character as an audition for his later part as James Bond; Ogilvy was dedicated to giving his version more depth of thought and feeling and man-of-action styling.

Simon grew up listening to girls laugh about his *lack* of style compared to the international elegance of the series, and the boys tried to challenge him to fights or climbing competitions; something that might prove his worthiness of the name of that man: The Saint, Simon Templar. He felt lucky to have had good

teachers and a few truly good friends, who intercepted the bad boys and made his school days turn out all right. And all those years of re-watching episodes of the original series and the reboot version hadn't prepared poor Simon for such a painfully undiluted moment of truth – like swallowing the red pill in *The Matrix* and realising the world you thought was real is a complete fake. Meredith had been shagging this Dean guy at the same time – although not *literally* at the same time – as she was shagging him. And now, on the brink of marriage to the love of his life, he felt like a gutted fish. A gutted fish forced to eat his own guts while all the other fish are laughing at him from the cool and safety of the water. A fish who thought he was a sleek trout, only to be revealed as a common, run-of-the-mill minnow.

'You, er, did know about Dean, didn't you?' Mark said. He seemed to sober up for a moment and looked at Simon, his eyebrows deepening to a furrow just above his eyes. Simon liked this man. He liked his own father too, regardless of the name faux-pas he had inflicted on his only son. How lucky he was to have two positive patriarchs. He looked at the expectant face of his future father-in-law, Mark's breath heavy with whiskey.

'Of course...Dean...yes. That was ages ago; another life. We're all over that now, Mark. I understand why she did what she did. Thought of doing something similar myself once or twice.' Simon winked, lied and forced a smile. A smile he noticed being reflected in the stark light of the mirror behind the bar. He looked away from himself quickly and back to Mark, who seemed satisfied with the answer.

'Did you *do* anything about that idea?' Mark said, sipping his whiskey. He was smiling, but the smile was waiting to unleash anger if Simon had been a cheater too.

'What do you mean *do anything*?' Simon knew exactly what Mark meant, but he was beginning to feel a heat at the back of his neck – the recognition of Meredith's betrayal. Images of this goddamn Dean and his fiancée; sex positions, lips wide with passion – Meredith forgetting her Saint, him back at home waiting for her to come in from *working late*...

'Did you ever play away from my little girl?' Mark was smiling now and *his* smile was full of weird trepidation – that this likeable young man, who he loved like a son, might turn out to be a creep too.

Simon wanted to burst in to screams and tears and blame Mark for the poor upbringing Meredith must have had, that she thought it was all right to sleep with two men at the same time; particularly when she had whispered words of deeply felt love in to Simon's ear and told him he was all she had ever wanted. That was just a lie, and maybe Mark – who forgave her this and anything else – had taught her that all was fair in love and war. Maybe it was Mark who Simon should be confronting? But he seemed so happy to be welcoming Simon into his family. Sainthood always came at a highly personal price.

The pub got busier and busier as Simon forced himself to chat with Mark about politics – although all he wanted to do was rush home and look into Meredith's sleeping face and try to find some trace of *real* love and humanity. Mark was vice-chairman of the local Conservative Party; Simon was a paid-up member of the New Labour Party. They played a game of *Pretend to Understand the Views of Someone you Disagree with Vehemently*. Simon was finally drunk. He had been trying to keep his senses clear – he usually hated the feeling of a swimming head and the resulting running at the mouth. He wasn't a cruel drunk, just a less-than-sensitive one and Meredith had often recounted embarrassing conversations at dinner parties – such as the time when Meredith's best friend, Judy, had dated a veteran of the 1991 Gulf War and Simon had spent an hour trying to draw information from the ex-

soldier on how many Iraqis he had killed, what it felt like to kill someone, and whether or not he had stashed away some Kuwaiti gold. Shameful moments.

Simon only had a vague memory of the evening; of making his usual unfunny reply-joke to Judy, saying she was looking for the perfect partner – some guy named Punch; of looking across the dining room table, which always rocked slightly and had to be propped on one of its legs by a cardboard wedge, and seeing Judy with a look on her face that said, 'Shut up. Shut up now.'

But he and Judy were friends and he had thought, at the time, that she was being sarcastic; mocking his words the way they both did to each other. He was mortified when he found out how crass he had been.

Simon nodded and pretended to listen to Mark's diatribe on how great the leadership of Margaret Thatcher had been – he kept his tongue wedged firmly in his cheek about *that* opinion. He thought about Judy. Had she known about Dean? She must have – she and Meredith were best friends. More betrayal.

'So, Mark, this Dean guy. When you met him, what did he look like? I mean, I knew about him but, for obvious reasons, I never actually saw him.' Simon smiled. He felt his face stiff with anguish and a cold sweat began to form at various points around his body – particularly the dribble that ran down his spine.

'Good looking young guy, bit full of himself. I guess he was *too* full of himself for Meredith. I mean she obviously liked him a lot, but I suppose she was more interested in someone like you ... someone responsible who would provide stability for her. Looks aren't everything, as the cliché goes.' Mark laughed at his own joke.

Simon found himself staring at Mark's brown teeth as he threw his head back. Did Mark have no empathy for Simon? Did he mean Simon wasn't good looking? Wasn't edgy? Wasn't the kind of cool guy that fathers hated? Damn that, he *wanted* to be hated by legions of dads the world over. Simon had a sudden vision of Dean as some kind of tanned muscle-Mary, skin-tight jeans, Cuban heels and a leather jacket like the ones worn by the T-Birds in *Grease*. In Simon's mind he had high cheekbones, hair pulled back like some Hollywood version of a Latino gangster, fragranced wet-look gel plastering each follicle. His teeth would have to be shiny white – maybe bleached and glow-in-the-dark. Simon had had teenage acne – pizza-face and Freddy Krueger were his classmates' favourite nicknames for him – highly unoriginal, but at the time they seemed like razor sharp insults, as if from the mouth of Oscar Wilde himself. He knew that Dean would never have suffered such an outcast-type fate in his existence. His skin would be smooth after every shave, no sign of any stubble. And he would certainly have a big tongue – like the satirical edition of Prince in his *Purple Rain* phase. Yeah, that would be about right; a huge tongue and he would work it like John Turturro as The Jesus in *The Big Lebowski.*

Oh god, this is a living death! Simon thought, I have to find this Dean guy and kill him slowly, and take his battered body back to Meredith; make her watch as I turn the corpse inside out, to *prove* I'm the better man; some kind of medieval ritual twisted in to my view of retribution.

He excused himself from Mark and went off to the toilets. He locked himself in a cubicle and sat on the toilet seat. He glanced at the graffiti on either side of him: *What you lookin' at ugly?!* greeted his eyes above the virtually empty toilet roll. How could he ever go through with the wedding now? She was a liar and a deceiver. His heart was broken in two flaking pieces, and yet he loved her too much to just give up hope. And the thing with Dean had been years ago. But then, if she had seen fit to cheat on him once maybe she had done it again and again...

He lifted the toilet seat, thought of slimy Dean and his tongue and vomited hard and fast. He sagged to his knees and groaned into the toilet bowl. After a few minutes he stood up and wiped his mouth, pulled a handful of the oddly damp toilet paper off the roll and pushed it behind his teeth. He clamped his lips shut – hoping the paper would soak up any residual vomit, held a hand across his mouth and screamed hard. A muffled sound echoed around the room. He punched the cubicle door a few times until his knuckles ached – with each connection he thought of Dean's face being smashed and bouncing back as if he was on a spring – the fluorescent teeth gleaming. A fairground 'laughing policeman' brought to life.

As Simon wandered back to the bar he saw Mark putting away his mobile phone. The stooped, older man downed more whiskey and it made Simon wonder if his future father-in-law might be an alcoholic.

'I'm leaving now,' Simon said, putting a hand on Mark's shoulder. Mark turned around quickly; almost spilling the remnants of his drink.

'Jesus, Saint, you nearly gave me a coroni ... coromo ... a heart failure thing. I was just on the phone to Merry, she didn't seem very pleased when I told her we'd been chatting about Deano. She was very quiet and told me I was a drunken fool and then put the bloody phone down on me. Bloody rude.'

Simon had lost the cuckold-martyr edge. Meredith knew exactly how he would be when he walked through the door later – she always had him figured out in any tough corner. It had previously made him feel comfortable; that she loved him so much she had taken the time to *really* know him like no other. But now it made him nauseous again; she would assume she could *handle* him in to submission and iron out the wrinkles of his hurt pride. She would have time to work out her excuses and time to call Judy to make their stories fit together. Simon drank the last of his whiskey. He had started on the booze later than Mark, and alternated with soft drinks, but his liver wasn't used to hard liquor and he was no match for Mark's drip-drip-drip of constant alcohol consumption. As he left the pub – Mark still propping up the bar and drinking – he felt smashed. His head span, his stomach flipped and flopped, and his mind struggled to cohere, coursing between his feelings of rage and confusion with Meredith and trying not to fall over.

Chapter 2...

He soon stopped, under an oak tree, and unzipped his flies. He watched as a trickle and then a streaming flow of urine fell to the grass just next to his shoes. Some of the urine splashed his shoes – beige suede Desert boots; brand new and now piss-stained. He thought of a scene, Dean laughing at him and pissing on him – Meredith laughing too and egging Dean on. Simon opened his eyes suddenly; a noise behind him.

'What the fuck you doin', mate?' an angry voice shouted.

Simon looked over his shoulder. Both his hands were clutching his penis – he had fallen asleep mid-urination; standing with his hips jutted out. There was a man, a huge man, coming towards Simon. He was holding something – a golf club.

'Piss on your own fuckin' tree, wanker,' the man said.

'What? Your tree? Wanker? Who? What?' Simon said. He looked at the face of the man – pure violence; he knew the man *would* use the golf club on him. His legs felt cold and tingly. He wanted to run but he was still holding his exposed penis. What should he do first: zip up or sprint away exposed?

'You wanker, piss on my tree, you bastard.'

Everything seeming to be happening in a slow motion of peril; Simon moved off the piss-soaked spot and began to run. He could feel his penis flapping up and down – as if it was waving – as he pounded along the pavement. He was still close to the pub – he knew the landlord through Mark and briefly thought of turning around and heading back that way. But that would mean risking golf club anger and how would he explain the exposed member?

After three attempts to zip up he finally managed the task; looking down and using both hands while running drunkenly at full speed wasn't an easy job. But, even in the fight-or-flightness of the moment he simply couldn't keep moving with his manhood on display. He stumbled and tripped; ran through puddles and leapt over a small wall. And then, even with the rush of wind in his ears and his breathing sounding like a supersonic jet, he realised he couldn't hear the voice of his potential attacker anymore. He looked back and the man was nowhere to be seen. Simon fell to his knees and began to cry. He began a conversation with himself.

'How, how can an evening begin with such hope and a sense of a good and bright future and then end with being told the woman you love has been shagging someone called Dean, and then you get chased down the street with your dick in your hands?'

He stopped crying and began to laugh: *'Ah ha, ha, ha!'*

The laugh had started as if he was in the role of a thigh-slapping pantomime dame. But the laugh was fake – something he thought he *should* be doing; as if he was in a film, laugh at the absurdity of it all, tomorrow was another day and all that bullshit.

But this wasn't a crucial scene and he wasn't the hero. No director would shout, *'Cut!'* and he would only have the filthy truth to face after these moments of alcohol-amplified reflection.

He had often thought – in such situations of stress, anger and fighting – that each life really should have a constantly running soundtrack. This evening called for *From a Late Night Train* by The Blue Nile: man on a late night train – no big surprise there – looking out through his reflected gloom, to the soggy cigarette butts and newspapers on a platform and realising that his love is over and that life is completely crap. Such a sad song that even the lead singer couldn't perform it live anymore – he had cried every time he attempted to bring it into the band's set. And even though Simon often listened to the track he always felt as if he were faking his response – sadness was expected as a reaction and that is how he felt. He knew he over-analysed; Meredith had found the characteristic sweet and individual when they first got together: "I love that you really think things through. I love that about you. Oh, that rhymes!" she had said, when first acknowledging his ability to observe and study and go over and over his innermost *issues* – yeah, great, he *was* Rodin's Thinker incarnate. Where had that got him?

And then, after one particularly drunken evening; as he began to talk through his thoughts and feelings about someone at the party they had been to, she turned on him and told him navels were for collecting fluff and that gazing upon them would give him a stiff neck and the inability to look forward. But then her credibility as an astute witness of human weakness had been eroded somewhat when that same evening she had vomited across their duvet and moments later in a post-vomit lust – who knew where that came from? – tried to French kiss him.

Simon stood up and brushed his trousers down. He remembered his thoughts from earlier – the idea that Meredith would be waiting for him, assuming her own supremacy in the area of emotional psychology and that she could use any means to win him over. She'd tell him that Dean was a passing thing; that they only dated a few times and never even slept together. She might even be making notes and placing those sisterly calls to

Judy – who, after the Gulf War soldier debacle, would be only too happy to conspire with Meredith.

'Fack you, Merry. Fack-a-doodle-do you,' he said, happy with his words and laughing aloud in the panto-fashion again. Walking on, he whistled and tried, in vain, to focus on the things around him – cars, trees, streetlights. He made mental notes, as if he would need to re-trace his footsteps. He stopped again. He didn't want or need to go straight home. Why give dear Merry the chance to win? He looked around and realised he was close to the home of his best friend, Sean. Sean would be exactly the right person to talk to about the deception. He would treat Simon's wounds and sympathise with him. Sean was *the man* for the job.

Simon hammered on Sean's front door. Sean answered quickly. Simon smiled at his friend and nodded. Sean looked surprised and then smiled back.

'Come on in, amigo mine,' Sean said.

'Thank you, my goof man. I mean, *good* man, ah, ha, ha.'

Simon walked in to the lounge half-expecting to see a young woman buttoning her blouse. Sean was an inveterate lothario. Simon had both admired his friend's way with women and yet wanted him to meet the *right one* – just like he had with Meredith. Oh, what a funny joke the concept of the *right one* seemed now; how fucking funny that really was. They would laugh and laugh at that.

'Didn't expect to see you this evening, Sim. I thought you and Marky Mark would be bladdered and having the "Treat my little girl well or I'll kill you" chat.

'Well, yeah, we *sort* of had that kind of chat. But the evening didn't exactly go that way. It was more ... eye opening than just the same old, same old,' Simon said. He couldn't understand why a large part of his personality was feeling *excited* at the thought of telling Sean about the Dean-deception. What kind of sick bastard was he that he was beginning to revel in the lies and feel empowered that he had taken a detour in his life – moved left instead of always right.

'What do you mean? I can see you're drunk, did you start telling the old git about your favourite sex acts with Merry? Or did you start lamenting over the fact that you can never have sex with another woman?' Sean was smiling; obviously waiting for an amusing tale of social humiliation.

Simon looked in to his friend's face; thought of Meredith and Dean naked together again and felt all excitement fade to nothing. But his moment of reality had come and in realising that he also knew that when he confronted Meredith he would have to end their relationship.

'Mark was pissed up, as usual, and he told me, in a matter-of-fact fashion, as if it was already common knowledge, that Merry had been shagging some guy for the first six months or so that we were together. Some guy called Dean. So ... it's all over, all down the drain, all blown to pieces, all fubar.'

'What the fuck? Hold on ... fubar?' Sean said, his eyebrows raised and his teeth clenched in question.

'Didn't you ever see *Saving Private Ryan*?'

'Of course. I saw it with you.'

'And you don't remember fubar?'

'Well obviously not.'

'Fucked up beyond all recognition.'

'Ah, yeah. Which character was talking about that?' Sean said, snapping his fingers wildly, as if that motion would bring about the vital cinematic answer.

This was how things went between the two of them in conversation: Digression-Central. Why hold one line of chat about a life-changing sequence of events that may ruin the way you view the opposite sex forever, when you can hold two and incorporate

cultural references as a way to solidify a friendship and mitigate the emotional pain?

'Shite, that's a tough one. I think the actor's called Adam something ... Adam ... the scene with the plane crashed and the march of the prisoners-of-war ... Adam ... Goldberg! He was in *Friends* too, played Chandler's nutter roommate, with the biscuit fish and the mannequin head for chips and dips.

'Yeah, yeah, right. And he was Julie Delpy's boyfriend in *Two Days in Paris*.'

'What?' Simon was remembering Billy Crystal and Debra Winger in a film that sounded like *Two Days in Paris*. Then he realised he was thinking of *Forget Paris*.

'Like a comedy version of *Before Sunrise* and the sequel ... also with la Julie lovely Delpy.'

Simon thought of Julie Delpy and wished he was engaged to her instead. She was beautiful and cool and funny and would never, as her character, Celine, have cheated on him. He had seen *Before Sunrise* in Paris with Meredith. At the time it had seemed to be the most romantic thing they could have done in the city. Meredith had placed her head on his shoulder as the film began and, even though he ached and wanted to move her halfway through the movie, he had felt very much loved in the darkness of that foreign cinema. It was their first holiday together. Five months into their relationship. He realised she had been seeing Dean during that time. Had she been thinking of *him* as she wiped tears of love and joy from her eyes as the end credits rolled? Had she wanted to take *him* back to the hotel and make love madly; as if the Apocalypse was waiting at reception for them to finish?

'So, anyway, fuck me sideways and call me Sally. What the fuckerooni is Meredith doing, or what *was* she doing, and who the fuck is this Dean guy?' Sean said, as if he was an echo from Simon's thoughts.

'I don't know, to all of those questions and a lot more. She's killed me, mate. This is the worst goddamn thing that's ever happened to me,' Simon said, feeling a new *reality* in his words and also feeling satisfied the he wasn't faking anything this time.

'Even worse than that time you chatted that girl up, got her number and left twenty messages on her machine and then eventually she called you back and told you never to call her again, all in the same evening?'

'Yes, even worse than that, but thanks for mentioning another humiliating moment of my life.'

'Even worse than *Gangs of New York*?'

'Yes, gee fucking whiz, worse than *that,* and remember Scorsese did at least try and make that *authentic*. Anyway, why the smart arse references?'

'Just trying, and apparently failing, to take your mind off the worst news you've ever had, fella,' Sean smiled weakly. Simon leaned towards him and lightly punched his shoulder.

'Thanks, man. I need this chat. Fuck Merry. Champagne for my real friends and real pain for my sham friends. Shall we watch something?'

'Sure, perhaps *25th Hour* after that Edward Norton quote. But, first, I was wondering if I could write a quick song about this?'

'This what?' Simon was beginning to sober up.

'This situation you find yourself in ... the heartbreak and all of that. What do you say?'

Sean often chose odd moments to compose a new lyric or melody. He had always claimed he had to go with whatever muse life handed him and just pick his guitar up and create.

'Yeah, go for it, this evening is a rolling nightmare, so let's keep rolling with it. Drink?'

'Vodka's in the freezer, mi amigo,' Sean shouted through to

the kitchen. Simon found the bottle and poured two large glasses. Sean was tuning his guitar as Simon returned to the lounge.

'Good evening, Wembley!' Sean said and smiled as he prepared himself. Simon sat back on the bamboo sofa; always uncomfortable.

'This one is for the lovers who have already lost,' Sean said dramatically and winked at Simon.

The song was written in ten minutes. Simon couldn't help smiling, although he *did* feel as if he was faking the smiles again, as Sean made appalling rhymes: Meredith – dirty dish, Dean – keen, unseen, a has-been and Simon – timing.

'What do you think, a hit maybe?' Sean asked, putting his guitar away and sitting back with his glass of vodka, like a man who has satisfied his deepest cravings.

'Of course. Who can't relate to a lying, cheating bitch who shags two people because she was taught it's all right to feel entitled to choice in all things,' Simon was shouting. He stopped himself and sat back. 'Sorry.'

'It's okay. It's *all* going to be okay too. Fuck it and fuck her ... and definitely fuck that Dean guy. Who the fuck, apart from Dean Martin who was the coolest Rat Packer, who calls their kid Dean?'

'Someone with low self-esteem. Hey, that rhymes with Dean, sort of. You should use that in your song,' Simon said and grinned.

'What do you fancy watching?'

'*Face-off*, I think. I know Nic Cage and Johnny Travolta are laughable and John Woo brings all his worst kind of action movie cliché into play, but I'm in the mood for that kind of violent fantasy bollocks.'

'I'm in too, my man. Let's take our faces ... off ...er,' Sean said, obviously trying to replicate the film dialogue. Simon smiled at him and shook his head.

'Now that *is* truly laughable,' he said. Sean gave him the middle finger, smiled back and opened the DVD case.

Simon tried to concentrate on the film – and the high octane noise, slow-motion agitated doves and scene chewing of the two lead actors was difficult to ignore – but he kept thinking about Meredith and Dean; trying to replay the first six months of his relationship – words, moments, promises made – over and over. Trying to see through the superficiality of new love, new sex and the way people try to present the best version of themselves to their new partner, especially when it seems there is a chance something *special* might grow into a commitment – a commitment like the proposal to Meredith to which she had replied with the Molly Bloom quote she had memorised: "... yes I said yes I will yes ..."

There was one distinct memory he managed to clarify from their first six months – a walk in the local nature reserve. The way Meredith had suddenly changed in her mood – from chatty and happy and trying to name various types of tree, to a shift into the sullen side of her personality. She remained quiet until later that evening. The information about trees hadn't registered with him: *deciduous?*

All he had noticed was the way she seemed to shine and he felt lifted away from any past worries or sense of not feeling at one with the world. For him, regardless of a happy childhood, his teenage angst had clung like a leech in to his early twenties. But Meredith had purged him and driven him headlong into that wondrous land called *Optimism*.

He couldn't remember what he had said – he thought he had mentioned how glad he was to have finally met someone who shared the same interests he had and who wanted the same things, a bit of a white lie about how much he liked the trees. But hey, he did like nature: browning leaves, the sight of a dog digging a hole and then chasing a hare, all of that was great.

He had wondered at the time if he had made a huge mistake;

applying too much pressure to their affair too early on, and as a consequence he had filled his mind with a vow to keep things happy and casual between them until she decided she was relaxed enough within herself to open up to him. He hadn't wanted to blow his chances with her. So many times with so many other women – usually subjects of unrequited love that he was friends with and never actually asked out – he would say or do something and watch as their faces changed from vague interest in what he was saying to an uncomfortable drop of realisation – he wanted to be their *boyfriend. Quelle horreur!*

He had felt, at the time, that any wrinkles in their blossoming union were his fault. And there was absolutely zero satisfaction in learning now that he had been wrong about that and about everything else. She had probably been feeling guilty or under unspoken pressure to make a choice between the two men in her life.

'Hey! No dropping off,' Sean's voice, loud and stroppy invaded his ears. His eyes shot open and he looked at his friend.

'What? What's the problem?' Simon said. He looked at his watch – a quarter past twelve.

'You fell asleep.'

'No shit. It's late, I'm still a bit pissed and my life sucks.' Simon wet his lips and blinked. He sat up and ran his hands through his hair.

'But you missed the end of the film, and I could barely hear it with your snuffling and snoring. I don't know how Merry ...' The two friends paused and remained silent for a moment. 'Do you want to stay in the spare room?' Sean said.

Simon nodded and smiled.

'Have you called Merry to let her know you're here?'

'Nope and I'm not going to either. I'll go home in the morning, make her suffer a sleepless night. Who knows, she might give ol'

Deano a call to come over and keep her warm.' Simon looked at his mobile phone – no missed calls; no text messages received. What the hell; NO contrition! Did she think she had been justified? Was she content to let him wander home thinking the worst? Or was she so upset inside her lies that she simply couldn't find the right words?

'Ah, the spirit of forgiveness is deep within you.'

'Fuck forgiveness. I've been a fool, a trusting idiot. She might have been messing around year after year. I guess I'm not enough for her. Has she ever flirted with you?'

Sean shifted and looked disgusted. He shook his head.

'No, no way. If she had tried that crap on me I'd have told you. Listen, mate, I'm no fan of deception. I always try, at least, to be honest with people and she probably does too. She was probably chewed up with indecision about her life and wanted to be sure about which way to go. And she chose you, not this Dean wanker. She chose *you*. I know you're hurt and feeling fucked over, but please think about what you're going to do. This is your whole life we're talking about.'

'Thanks. Listen, I'm knackered and going to bed. I just wanted to check something with you. If this thing with Merry does go south, can I stay here for a while?'

'Always, mate. Of course,' Sean said.

Chapter 3...

The next morning Simon woke early. He was the manager of a small bookshop and in the privileged position of not having to provide any proof of illness on the rare occasions when he took

a sick day. He called the shop and his assistant manager, Marion, answered almost immediately.

'The Written Word, good morning,' she said.

'Morning, Maz, it's me. I woke up feeling awful, my temperature's up too. I won't be in today. I'll call you in the morning if I'm not going to make it tomorrow. Okay?'

There was a pause. Marion detested illness at work and, to Simon's recollection, hadn't taken a single sick day in the five years they had worked together.

'That's fine. Actually, Meredith just called to ask if you were in yet. Where exactly are you, especially if you're so ill?'

Simon pulled a face, which resembled someone realising they're standing in the middle of a crowded street with no clothes on.

'I left the house early to get a doctor appointment before work. I didn't want to wake Merry. I did leave her a note; she must have missed it. Anyway, you're beginning to sound as if you don't believe me.'

Simon was remembering the previous evening – every indignant moment – and he felt a pulse of angry energy course through his body. Who the hell did Marion think she was to question him? He was in charge, not her. He had promoted her.

'Sorry. I was just a bit concerned about you. I'll be fine. You take it easy and get well soon. Anything in particular you want done today?'

'I leave that to you. I'm off back to bed. Bye.'

'Bye.'

Simon went downstairs. Sean had already left for work. He was also a retail manager. He ran a musical instrument shop. He often told Simon it made him feel as if he was truly close to his goal of becoming a singer-songwriter.

Sean *had* left a note:

Merry called early. Speak to her. Later.

Simon looked at his mobile phone: 4 messages. 3 missed calls. All Meredith. He had put his phone on to silent mode just before he fell asleep – with the vague thought that Meredith might call and that he didn't want to speak to her on her terms, only when he was good and ready.

His right index finger hovered over the phone. He was shy of the messages. What if she had had time to decide *he* wasn't worth the fight to stay together? What if she was saying he had to move out ASAP? Or worst of all, that she was still seeing Dean and had decided to marry him instead?

Simon stared in to empty space for a moment or two, then made himself a cup of coffee. His left eye began to twitch. He had been prescribed beta-blockers for the same condition a year or so before and the doctor had diagnosed irregular heart rhythms due to stress. And, man alive, he was stressed now. And where were the beta-blockers when he needed them? At home with Meredith. He clutched his face, pulling his left eyelid down and holding the twitch firmly still. He walked to the mirror in the hallway and looked at his face – dark sacks of sleeplessness under his eyes; his face almost afraid of its own reflection in the morning light.

'What the fuck am I going to do?' he said to himself.

His phone rang. Meredith calling again. He looked at the display screen, paused and drew breath, then answered the call.

'Hello.'

'Simon?'

He wanted to say, 'No, it's Dean here. I've stolen Simon's phone and his girl!' But instead he said, 'Yes, it's me. Good morning, Meredith.' He only used her full name when things between them were "less than great" – the phrase Meredith liked to use to explain things to her mother during their Sunday morning phone chats.

'How are you this morning?' she said.

How was he? How did she think he was? He was empty, floating on the currents of hopelessness, lost in the ether of despair. And he was hungry. The smell of burned toast still filled the air downstairs and he wanted a slice.

'I'm okay. Tired and hungry, but okay. How are you?' He sounded happy. He was so happy that he *sounded* happy. She must be squirming, he thought. He liked the sense of being in charge of the phone call; so unexpectedly, so quickly too. He had half-expected that he would be open to her words and charms – like Mowgli to the snake Kaa in *The Jungle Book*.

'I feel like shit. I *am* shit, Simon. I want you to know that *I* know what I've done to us and I also know it's too early to decide how things ...'

'Let's not talk now. We can't really discuss this ... I need time to think and get my head around this mess. I'll call you later. Bye.'

'But, I ... okay. Oh, Simon, I'm truly sorry ... Bye.' She sighed as before she put the phone down.

Simon sat down, the bamboo frame of the sofa digging into his lower back. He sat forward, sipped his coffee and thought about her words; the cadence of her voice – complete contrition and desperation. He suddenly stood up and grabbed for his mobile phone again. What was he doing?! He was missing a chance to talk, arrange things, plan for the future...

But he managed to stop himself from simply falling in line with what he assumed were her plans. Perhaps he had handled things perfectly well and he should do what he told her – think things through; take his time and consider everything. He was only twenty-six years old; tall, slim and, or so he had thought, reasonably attractive. He had been told by one ex-girlfriend – admittedly one who was a huge Fleetwood Mac fan and thought Stevie Nicks was *mystical* – that he had the same profile as the

1930s film actor John Barrymore, who had starred with Greta Garbo in *Grand Hotel*.

That had sounded like a wonderful compliment until Simon had started to read about Barrymore. The actor had a striking jaw-line that said *class* and looks of intelligence and wisdom. And then he read that Barrymore had eventually succumbed to alcoholism and a permanent state of confusion.

Simon slumped back on the sofa again and thought of himself as always at the back-end of love. Self-pity wasn't an asset, but with a hangover and a car-crash life he allowed himself to indulge.

He opened the file photos on his mobile phone and flicked through various disorganised shots of Meredith – in bed, by the cooker, close-up to the camera with her tongue hanging out. He smiled and wanted to touch her face; the photos were the closest he could get right there and then, and he found himself stroking the screen of his phone; silence finally broken by his stomach rumbling.

'Good goddamn, I need toast and I need it now,' he said and ran to the kitchen. He looked for the toaster – Sean was obsessive about keeping his kitchen work-surfaces clear and clean. He would disinfect them at least twice a day and scrub them until he almost broke a sweat. Simon ignored the obsessive compulsive side of his best friend; in truth the two of them ignored all and any negativity in the other and they made certain they *never* argued and stayed on safe subjects: Sean's women, film, music, etc. Meredith constantly berated Simon for not having a "good, real world chat" with Sean.

Eventually he found the toaster; then the bread – wrapped in four layers of plastic and on the second shelf of the fridge; far enough away from the equally heavily wrapped raw meat on the bottom shelf.

Simon plugged his earphones in to his iPod and found a

collection of Crowded House. The first track *Weather With You* drifted by without him really noticing – familiarity with the lyrics, chorus, melody and the rest had taken away any new feelings towards the tune. But the next track, *Better Be Home Soon* made him stop and listen as if he was being held by the song of the Siren, about to be dashed on the rocks. He turned up the volume to maximum and sat at the kitchen table. He crunched the buttery bread and listened to the song another couple of times, taking care to really hear every lyric. Then he took the earphones out and picked up his mobile phone again. He pressed a button for speed dial.

'Simon?' Meredith's voice was full of happy enquiry.

'Yeah, it's me again, the sucker in your life. We need to talk. We need to meet and talk as soon as we can.' The fake happiness in his voice from the earlier phone call had vanished.

'Okay. I've phoned in sick to work, same as you. Do you want to come back home and talk now?'

'Sure. I'll get dressed and catch a bus. I'll see you in a bit. Bye.'

'Bye. I love you.'

'Bye.'

The 'I love you' had come like a bullet to his chest – he felt like Neo in *The Matrix*, falling backwards; holding his body above the ground; dodging the onslaught of munitions. He felt sick. His stomach churned. He sent Sean a text:

> Going home to talk to Merry. Feeling like I'm going to hurl. What did Wayne and Garth decide in Wayne's World about a girl seeing you throw up and staying with you? Was good to see you, mate. Feeling fucked up about this forthcoming edition of the Chat About Having Sex With Other People showdown with Merry. Text you later.

Chapter 4...

Simon walked up to his own front door and wondered, if only for a second or two, whether he should knock before going in. He made a face of disgust at his own lack of courage and purpose and tried to pull his keys out of his jacket. The jacket was old and needed patches on the elbows and the lining of the pockets was full of holes. His keys caught on one of the holes and he had to yank and pull; push and twist to release the bunch.

'Fucky, fucky, bugger,' he stage-whispered. And then Meredith opened the door, and he thought he *would* hurl.

'Hi, Sim. Come on in,' she said, in a voice of composure. She was dressed in a long summer skirt – pale green linen – and a light blue blouse. She looked very beautiful. Her light blonde hair was put up at the back; a single lock dropped in front of her eyes and she pushed it behind her ear.

He knew if he looked at her for too long any resolve to discuss the issues and force confession from her would dissolve into the same hopeless wave of love he had always felt. He had heard the film director Anthony Minghella use the word uxorious about his wife when he collected his Best Director Oscar for *The English Patient*. He had looked the word up: *adoration for a wife* was the description. He had felt that way about Meredith since they met – married her in his heart the first time they kissed.

He suspected she would be going in to work later. She was in marketing and PR at the local council. She was a careerist and he usually liked that in her; it had inspired him to work hard and harder for the bookshop management position. They had a long-running, unspoken, competition to out-earn each other. Meredith was in front with the highest salary these days. He was proud of her.

But on this day he didn't care about jobs or money or ambition. He looked at her and thought of Dean and that was all – about the lies and the sweaty sex: *that* tongue – like Jabba the Hutt in *Return of the Jedi* licking Princess Leia – came in to his mind again. He closed his eyes and forced the image away, and the way he had been left hanging over the side of the cliff of being dumped for months; when he thought they were in the throes of exploding love: *l'amour fou.* And even before he had spoken a word to her about how they might try and regain trust, re-build their life together and eventually marry, he knew it was all over. That damn Blue Nile song began to play in his mind again.

He tried to change the head-track, but the song and the sentiment was locked in.

'Would you like a cup of tea?' Meredith asked him.

'Yes, please. Thanks. Are you going to work later?' he said. He followed her through to the kitchen.

'I might have to, yes. I've got to finish a release for the council leader. I ...'

She clicked the on-switch and the kettle began to boil. They stood in silence until the tea was made – half-smiles at each other to maintain a sense of familiarity and domestic comfort. Simon felt the only way he could cope with the scene was, as usual, to compare what he was going through with a film; try to pretend he was acting and that nothing could touch him emotionally. Perhaps Rick and Ilsa in *Casablanca* – the uncomfortable recognition throughout the film that the intensity of their love, although never diminished, has been put on indefinite hold due to the re-emergence of the heroic and handsome freedom-fighter, Victor, played by the matinee idol Paul Henreid. The central idea of the tragedy of love filled Simon's head – cigarettes being smoked seductively; chiaroscuro images and couples giving up any hope of being happy to do "the right thing".

He snapped back to reality and looked at Meredith. This wasn't a particularly cinematic moment. The kitchen bin needed emptying – he usually looked after that – and the way Meredith left the teabags lying in the kitchen sink bothered him too. Could she not just put them in the food composter? Its function was obvious; it actually stated on the side: *Yes, you can put teabags in this bin.*

He sipped his tea and nodded a thank you to her; made his way back to the lounge and thought of other things she consistently failed to do: close the downstairs toilet door properly; replace the handsoap dispenser...

'Sim, Simon ... I love you *so* much. You need to know that. I know this is awful for you, especially finding out the way you did from my loud-mouth dad. The thing is, there aren't *any* excuses for this. I don't know how to start explaining the whole mess. I was scared and selfish and not old enough to believe I had found everything I would ever need when I first met you. I knew Dean from college, we had dated a few times, and it just kept going for a while after you and I began ... '

'Began what? Fucking?' Simon was surprised at the tone in his voice – sarcasm. He didn't feel sarcastic. He felt as if he was on fire; burning slowly, smoke rising from underneath his shirt and that he was too self-conscious to mention the fact to anyone.

'Well, yes, that, and after we began to get serious. I ...'

'Sorry, do you mean, after you and Dean got serious or you and I?'

'You and me, obviously,' Meredith replied, sounding annoyed. She bit her top lip and sipped some tea.

'It's *not* all right to feel pissed with me because I'm asking what you assume are leading or stupid questions, Merry. I'm not being obtuse about this shitty situation. I feel empty right now. I feel completely twisted and wrecked. You have ruined my life.'

Simon regretted the *ruined my life* line. He was faking that

emotional position again. She had upset him and made him feel dirty and small; covered in the stinking downpour of her lie. But she hadn't ruined him and he knew he could recover in some way. But, as he watched tears begin to form in her eyes, he was glad for making such a serious claim. He wanted her to suffer, if only for a short time. Surely that was fair?

Meredith went to the bathroom and wept for a while. Simon stood near the door and heard her deep sighs – she always tried not to make a noise when she cried; whereas he had a tendency to make a loud sob on those few occasions when turns in his life had been deeply unpleasant.

He felt awful for his cruelty. The conversation in his mind was oscillating: the positives of his behaviour – honesty and sticking up for himself against the most negative assaults – against Meredith in tears, his angry-energy beginning to seep away on the foreknowledge that he would never be able to forgive her anyway and that they were merely wasting time in the death throes of the relationship. How was he supposed to start again? He cringed, the Michael Bolton track, *How Am I Supposed to Live Without You* began to play in his thoughts; the most loathsome song and in such a personally tragic moment. He stared into space, willing himself to find another song, a happy place. Marc Bolan singing *Metal Guru* but only for a second, then that damn Bolton git again. Why had he thought of Bolan? He died young in a car-crash. He tried to regain the tune, but that power ballad held tight. He wondered if things might get even worse; Celine Dion wailing *My Heart Will Go On* might invade his brain and finally push him into a hideous process of holding Meredith to his chest and telling her it was all okay.

The lock on the bathroom door broke through his musical tortures; he sprinted back to the lounge. This is absurd, he thought, taking his sofa seat back and picking his tea mug off the floor.

Meredith walked in to the lounge and sat opposite him. Her eyes were red. She smiled at him. He smiled back.

'What do you want to do about this?' she asked him.

'Why do I have to decide what we should do?' Simon felt his face begin to grow hot with the stress of it all.

'Because I don't have any right to try and dictate to you. I knew this would come out one day. I just hoped I would be able to tell you in my own way; my own time. I always put it off because we were happy and I didn't want to lose you. I don't want to lose you now.'

'Well, that's great. The road to hell ... blah, blah ... intentions were good and all that jazz. Merry, I loved you so much. I still do. That isn't the problem. The problem is I don't trust you now. I know I can be a dickhead. I know I have a huge number of annoying character flaws, but betrayal isn't one of them. And, to me, it's one of the worst. Maybe the worst of all.'

'So ... you're breaking it all off?' she asked. Meredith looked at him with eyes that were pleading for clemency.

'Why did you bother *trying* out the two of us, this wanker Dean and me? Wasn't it exhausting lying to two people all the time? I just don't understand why you couldn't do what virtually everyone else does and take a chance on just the one. Two-timing is the kind of thing a thirteen year old might do.' Simon said the words and noticed Meredith with *that* look on her face again. The look of the self-righteous. He waited for her to start justifying her deception; to begin the framing of her life and the context of need and want, and how she had to know, really *know,* that Simon was the man for her. He was mentally ready to leap on her words and crush them with cold facts. He knew he was guessing about her thought process, and he certainly wasn't feeling objective.

He tried for a moment to be like William Holden in *Sunset Boulevard*; not the bit about being dead, floating on the surface

of a Beverley Hills swimming pool; but the part about the post-traumatic ability to see clearly through the horror of the situation you are in; to realise the insanity of the person you are confronting and that in some way you have been complicit in their madness too. And that you can be released from the stasis and float away to a hopeful future.

'Are you leaving me, Simon?' she asked.

He knew the answer was: yes, yes, yes. But he couldn't bring himself to say it immediately. He wanted to be wrong. He wanted to wipe his mind and begin again, like a *Stepford* wife; just being compliant and avoiding the difficulty of the truth.

'So?' Meredith said. She looked at her watch.

'Yes. Yes, I am leaving. I'm going to live with Sean for a while. But I do want to try and sort this out.'

'Sort what out?' Meredith was sounding more and more impatient.

'Well, I *really* don't know, Merry.' Simon's face was burning with annoyance. He wanted to launch his tea mug at the wall, but they had only just finished decorating the lounge – a terracotta colour paint; they had used sponges to give a distressed impression. 'Maybe we could sort out global warming; cover the sky in tinfoil. Maybe we could sort out world poverty by getting everyone to have donate their spare change with the rubbish collections each week. Jesus Christ, Merry. Sort out the shit *you've* put us in.'

'Just go if you're going.'

'Right. Okay. It's like that, eh? You get to fuck someone else and I end up being the bad guy?' Simon knew he was losing any position of martyrdom he may have had at the start of the conversation and he knew he was whining. He had a flashback of being a child, maybe aged six or seven; of throwing his head back in frustration with his parents and groaning. He felt ridiculous.

'Simon, I don't want to break up with you. I love you so very much. I want to spend the rest of my life with you and make amends for the pain I've caused you. But I won't have you bullying me. I *know* I've done something awful.'

Simon wanted to whine again – that it was his *right* to shout and scream and make her feel even worse. But *he* felt worse about wanting to hurt her. And he didn't want to leave her, but he knew he had to; if only to return and make her realise what she had nearly lost. Surely, in what Simon had always considered a Godless universe, and in the midst of the scenario he found himself in he could keep his options open; to leave and return was his *essential* role in this. He knew he was deflecting his own attention away from the awful resolution. He had told her he was going out of the door and now he had to actually walk away. He felt so at home – not that strange, as he was *at* home – and he took a second or two to glance around the house. He had been so happy when they bought the property, after a protracted battle with another couple to come up with the deposit and get the mortgage approved. The seller was a builder and an estate agent, and a grinning bastard who wanted more and more money and time from them. He reminded Simon of Alan Rickman as Hans Gruber in the original *Die Hard,* although nowhere near as debonair. They had finally won the keys and, in the middle of the first night in their new home, Simon had realised he felt, for the first time since he was a child, safe. Safe and loved.

He smiled to himself at the memory and then remembered they had bought the house within the first eighteen months of their relationship and he began to wonder if mean, lean Dean had still been on the scene. He blanched at the rhyme and looked at Meredith. She was staring at him harder than ever – waiting for his next move. The look on her face reminded him of many film noir scenes. He was the handsome hero settling a score with the femme fatale of the piece. She was that femme. He had the gun

aimed at her heart; she had ruined enough lives and she had it coming. Bogart would have been proud of him.

Simon smiled weakly. He leaned forward and took Meredith's hands. 'I love you, Merry. Nothing that's happened or is happening now is ever going to change that. The thing is, I need some time to deal with this, to process the anger and the pain. So I'm going to leave for a while.'

Later that day, Simon would have time to think about what he might have expected in Meredith's reaction – at the time he didn't have a moment to think or speak to himself about the possible consequences of his departure. He might have expected her to nod and wish him well and kiss his cheek; see him off at the front door and tell him: "Hurry home, my love". But there was only ever going to be acrimony. And when he looked back he knew he had handled the situation about as badly as it was possible and in the most sanctimonious way he could have.

'Fuck you, Simon Templar. You have no idea how bad I feel about this. I've ruined everything, but I have always been there for you. I've never asked you for anything, until now. I know forgiveness is hard and it takes time but I can't believe you won't even give me a chance!' Meredith screamed the words at him. He had never seen her so angry – usually she contained her extreme emotions; literally biting her lip to stop any flood of anger or resentment. She usually took her time to consider her – it made her job easier, she often said, and her life. Until now.

Chapter 5...

Simon reached the bus stop at the end of the road. He could still see the front of his house. Meredith had drawn the curtains.

He had half-expected to see her zoom by in her car, maybe sticking one of her middle fingers up at him and pushing her tongue out for extra effect, just as he had done at primary school to his most detested teacher and received five whacks of the slipper as a consequence. But he knew she was crushed. He had done the crushing; a full body-slam from the top of the metaphorical ropes in their life together, like some WWE goon covered in spandex. And he didn't like the feelings bubbling inside himself – a mix of anxiety, guilt and self-loathing.

Then he began to experience counter feelings of self-righteousness: standing by his words and deeds, like some Wild West hero; clip-clopping away on his trusty horse. But honestly, where did walking away ever get anyone – lonely, sitting and staring into the space where the one you love should be.

He tried to pull his mobile phone from his pocket – that damn pocket with the hole again; the phone had disappeared into the jacket lining. He delved ever deeper until his hand was near his back. He looked down at the shape of his fingers inside the material and thought of a sock puppet; like the sock puppets he and Meredith had made for a children's charity two years ago at Christmas; the best Christmas they had spent together. It wasn't that long until this next Christmas. He wondered if he would be spending it alone – such an awful thought. There wasn't anyone else waiting at the bus stop so he began a whispered conversation with the hand inside his jacket.

'So, hombre, you kind of fucked it all up, eh?' the hand said.

'Yup. I did. I can't believe I'm standing here like this, waiting to

go away, maybe for good,' Simon said.

'Well, it's your choice, amigo.'

'True enough, but the thing is, handy, old friend, I don't really feel anything in particular right this moment. I know I should have a clear sense of things: her, bad, me, good. But I don't feel that or anything else very much. Does that make me a weirdo?'

'No. What makes you a weirdo is talking to your own hand or anybody else's. What do you want to do now?'

'Watch a film. Get drunk. Talk to Sean later. And text something to Merry, something nice.'

'So do that. Do it all. Do it now. Which film?'

'Maybe I should track down that Michael Caine film, *The Hand*?'

'Ha ha, very good. They offered me a part in the sequel. Only trouble is, it's crap. Try *True Romance*, always a winner, one of your favourites and Tarantino's words always get you going.'

'Thank you and goodbye,' Simon said, quietly, as he pulled his hand out of his jacket, holding the mobile phone. Someone else had joined him at the bus stop. He looked at his hand and smiled. He began to write a text:

> Merry, hi, I'm still at the bottom of the street, waiting for a bus. I know you're upset with me. I'm sorry about that. Sorry doesn't even begin to cover what I feel for either of us. I don't really know what to think or how I should be feeling right this second. I do know I love you. I know people say that isn't enough. Maybe that's true, maybe it isn't, but it feels like a good place to start from. There are things I want to say; questions I want to ask, but I'm afraid I ...

And then Simon stopped for a moment to think of the best way to sign off his text. It had to be a classic example of stoicism and grace under emotional fire. Something that might make

Meredith clutch her mobile phone to her chest; heaving a sigh of contentment that she was still with a Man of Honour; a man who knew the value of decency and ... He realised he had pressed the *send* button by accident.

'Oh, shit that. Bugger, fucky fuck,' he said. He glanced at the young woman standing next to him; she smiled nervously back at him. Did he know her? Nice face, nice style of clothing, nice ... Oh shitty bugger, he thought, just re-focus. He was well aware he was behaving like the cliché of a nutter at the bus stop. He wondered if he should use his hand again – a diversion; another conversation to be had and maybe the hand might be able to help in his plight. Should he go back to the house and finish the last sentence of his text in person? How could he do that to her after leaving with such ceremony and bravado? It would probably appear as an act of great cruelty, the choice of a sadist. But he couldn't just leave her hanging like that, intrigued and confused by the end of his thought process, although he had his doubts about his own potential for intrigue.

He was beginning to realise he had probably said enough for one day and ramming home a point of order wasn't any use at all. He was grateful to his brain in situations like these; that he had the capacity to stop and think about ramifications.

'Are you all right?' a voice to his left caused him to begin the re-focusing.

'Sorry?' he said, looking at the young woman who had smiled nervously at him just a few minutes before.

'You seem a bit upset and you were talking to your hand.'

Oh. My. God! Simon thought, I have lost my mind. *The hand has got to go.*

'I was trying to remember something. I must have looked like a nutter at the bus stop cliché. Do I know you?' he said, narrowing his eyes because he thought he looked cooler that way – like Clint

Eastwood in *The Good, the Bad and the Ugly*. He turned his head to one side. He could see a vague reflection of himself in the bus shelter perspex window. He didn't look like Eastwood. He looked more like some poor unfortunate who has woken up with a stiff neck and a fly stuck to his eyeball.

'Not really. I've seen you at the badminton club on Sunday evenings.'

Simon smiled and nodded but had absolutely no memory of her. Had she been watching him as he danced around on the court – whacking the shuttlecock; diving here and there and generally being overly competitive?

'Do you live around here?' he asked. His mind had gone blank – do *I* live around here, where is *here* in this town?

What the hell was he supposed to be saying at this moment? He had just left his home; maybe for the last time and now he was engaging in what his dad called "Playful banter" with another woman. A really lovely looking woman who was not Meredith. Was it all right to be talking to her after walking out on his fiancée? His face was growing hot and red again, and his armpits were getting wetter and wetter. He was attracted to this woman! To her face, her voice and her body. The love of his life was less than one hundred metres away; probably sobbing over a photograph of the two of them, and here he was trying to flirt – and making a terrible job of it. He knew Clint Eastwood would be clutching his head in shame at such a sight.

'Just up the road.' The young woman turned and pointed at a group of houses on the other side of the park next to them. 'Is that your girlfriend you usually go to badminton with?' she asked. Simon was about to say yes, and then he took a moment. *Was* Merry still his girlfriend? Or were they "on a break" like Ross and Rachel were/weren't in *Friends*?

'No. She's a good friend,' he lied.

He had stepped out of his life. He thought about apologising and walking away; only thinking about Merry and how they could re-build their life, but that just didn't feel right. It felt like damp compromise. He focused his mind: *Dean, Dean, Dean.* He fought down any feelings of anxiety about this flirtation. He had always played fair. He had always been called *good.* But *this* was feeling good. It felt scary, a bit painful in his stomach, but exciting. Very exciting. 'How very rude of me, I haven't introduced myself. My name's Simon Templar.' He held out his hand; hoping the palm wasn't too cold and clammy.

'Sarah Marshall,' she replied. She shook his hand. Her light touch and the smoothness of her skin made Simon want to curl in to an "Aw, shucks" moment of smiling and cooing.

'Simon Templar? Wasn't that the name of the guy in that television programme about a spy?' Sarah asked him.

'Yes it is the same name. My damn dad and his stupid 1970s drug-addled ideas. Mind you, the show wasn't really about spies, people often make that association because Roger Moore was the first Saint and he played James Bond later, so ...' Simon's detailed exposition trailed off. Sarah nodded and smiled, but her smile seemed to be full of kind disinterest.

'So I was wondering whether you'd be interested in meeting for a cup of coffee of something? My bus will be here soon but I'd love to meet and chat again,' Sarah said. She was shrugging and blushing. She looked adorable.

Would he be interested in taking a whole new turn in his existence? He looked at Sarah. She was smiling at him. Surely this wasn't real. Maybe Meredith knew Sarah from the badminton club and she had called her from the bathroom earlier. Maybe they had arranged to test him at the bus stop to see how far he would go in his lust for revenge? But that must be wrong, he thought, how would Merry know I would be catching a bus?

'I *would* be interested, very interested in mating you, I mean meeting you for coffee,' he said. He grinned and felt his face glow ever hotter in the word-error aftermath.

Mating! Mating? How could he have said that? He felt as if the humiliation in his life had reached its zenith – he certainly hoped so.

He looked in to Sarah's face and expected to see a: *I'm talking to a psychopath!* expression appear. Or perhaps a look of utter disgust. After all, he didn't have the confidence to assume she saw him as anything more than a new friend. A weird friend with some form of sexual Tourettes Syndrome. And a fondness for hand chats.

Sarah's face didn't drop into a look of fear or betray even a blink of surprise. Instead her mouth began another smile, and then she began to laugh.

'That was very funny, mating and then meeting. That was very witty,' she said. She touched his arm. He smiled back and laughed. He thought of Joe Pesci in *Goodfellas:* "Do I amoose you? ... funny how? ... funny like a fuckin' clown?' But *he* wasn't a psychotic Mafia enforcer like Pesci's character and he was just elated Sarah had seen the funny side of his mix-up – that she was so easy-going and happy to believe in the best of him.

'That's my bus coming,' she said. 'Do you have a mobile? I'll give you my number.'

Simon tapped in the digits and saved them. He waved Sarah goodbye and looked back at his house – curtains still drawn; no sign of Meredith leaving. Perhaps she would work at home, send the relevant work in by email and go to bed early. Or maybe she would go in to work, stay late, go to the local pub, where she would meet up with colleagues; sit next to some guy, maybe Ian from Council Tax collections, get drunk and end up in bed with him as a "Fuck you and goodbye" to their relationship?

Simon closed his eyes tightly and jogged on the spot. He would go insane thinking like that. And then Simon thought of Sarah; how nice it had felt talking to someone new, someone not yet polluted by the fumes of an old/dying/not-quite-working-as-you-hoped-it-would relationship. They had connected. Simon had made a hideous mistake, basically telling her he wanted to have sex with her; and she had laughed it off. How great were the beginnings of relationships? So great that Simon began to wish he could have a new beginning every day. Well, maybe not every day, that would be exhausting and boring; re-hashing the same tired lines, and some lies, about who you are and what you do; what your parents are like and trying to work out if the other person likes you or not. But if he could find a way to have a new beginning of some kind to look forward to every so often that *would* be great. Maybe there was a way to have a new beginning, a reanimating, in his relationship with Meredith? The relationship wasn't *officially* dead, although moving out didn't exactly send a message of happy lovers with a golden future.

The relationship was now frozen in time; caught in the first six months forever; when Meredith could have changed everything – dumped Dean and truly committed to Simon. Instead she had hedged her bets, played the field and utilised all the other clichés which amounted to *lies damn lies*.

Simon caught his bus and sat back to think about how long he should wait before he called Sarah. A day? Two days? A week? Twenty-five minutes? What was dating-industry standard these days? Was there an industry standard?

He texted Sean:

Loads to tell you. On my way back to yours, need a bed for a bit longer. Hope that's coolio. Quickie question: how long are you supposed to wait before you call a woman, when you've just met?

He pressed send and a reply came back with minutes:

WTF? You bet you've got loads to tell me. What's with the calling a woman? Which woman? Merry? Can't be her of course, you said you just met. When and where did you meet? Going mad with questions here! Don't call ANY women until we talk, not even your mother! Of course you can stay. Let's make a list of must-see movies to watch during your stay. My suggestion to start things off is Swingers, baby! Gotta have a classic about young male insecurity and bravado to begin things, eh?
And remember, as Dean Martin sang, "You're nobody till somebody loves you ..." Sorry about referencing someone called Dean ...

Simon texted Sean back:

Swingers sounds good. Feeling a lot like Mikey in the film too. Do I still have claws to kill the bunny? Am I the bunny? Talking a lot of crap today. Feeling seriously fubar again, things awful with Merry. You do remember fubar don't you? Ha ha. Later.

Sean replied quickly:

Fubar you are. And yes, I do realise that doesn't even make any sense. Later to you too.

Chapter 6...

Simon had a spare key to Sean's house. He had been given one on the third occasion Sean was burgled; each time during a family holiday – Sean's parents were very rich and treated him to foreign climes each year. Simon had become a security blanket for Sean, checking the house each day, moving post away from the front door and checking the various locks and light-timer switches.

Simon let himself back in to the house. The curtains were still drawn in the lounge; he pulled them back and let the light in. He sat back on the uncomfortable sofa and breathed out heavily – so much *action* in so little time. Just a day ago he had been completely oblivious to the maelstrom waiting just around the corner, waiting to mug him and drag him into the undertow of numb recognition that the life he thought he had was a complete illusion. He wondered for a moment if he had just been a yardstick to Meredith; a way for her to feel as if she had achieved the relevant steps towards becoming a responsible adult. That maybe she had considered the entire episode with Dean and him as being akin to a social experiment of sorts; a way of discovering her true identity. How terribly *cosmopolitan* of her, how terribly, terribly Happy Valley in Kenya in the 1930s; the Bohemian upper-crust-ness of it all. What a jolly lark!

He pulled his mobile phone out and looked at Sarah's number. He looked away and back at the phone, and then he began to write her a text message:

Hi, it's me, Simon Templar, already ...

He stopped and deleted the words so far and began again:

Hi, Sarah, it was so good to meet you today. I was having a really bad day and ...

He stopped again and deleted the second effort. And then began again:

Hi, Sarah, my name is Templar, Simon Templar – you might remember me, good-looking guy, five-ten height – and I think

you look gooood in red. I really enjoyed touching bust, I mean base. Ha ha, just like mating and meeting!

He smiled and cleared the mess of words. He often played what he and Sean called Russian Roulette Texting: a game of writing a text containing all the things you might want to say to someone you are either attracted to or dislike a lot – being completely frank and honest to the point of cringing, then opening the contacts page, closing your eyes, letting your index finger fall on the phone. Simon had sent three texts that way and had to quickly follow them with apologies and detailed explanation that he had sent the text to the wrong person. Sean had sent a lot more than that and never followed up with any apologies. But then Sean had the freedom of money and the single-guy life and just didn't give a damn.

'Just say something casual, something good and interesting and something that won't make her think you are the new Hannibal Lecter,' Simon said to himself. He began to tap letters in to his phone again and then stopped suddenly – a rush of panic filled him. What if he sent this text to Meredith! How *B A D* would that be?! He would have to watch *every* movement of his fingertips; check each word, name and number. He still had the upper-hand, albeit a strained one that he didn't enjoy talking to – he hadn't exactly left Meredith thinking he was the all-round good-guy, forgiving of sexual indiscretions and open to aimless reconciliation.

He knew that one hint of infidelity on his part and his position in the relationship might even appear weaker than hers. Meredith could always claim youth, naivety and fear of making a mistake with her heart as the reason for the Dean-thing. But he would just look like a creep, a loser – *the* guy from the Radiohead song.

'Type that mo-fo with care, my friend,' Simon said to his hand.

The hand nodded back at him in the shape of a duck's head.

Simon narrowed his eyes, again thinking of Clint Eastwood – *he* never had to worry about mobile-mishaps in his classic films. The Man-with-no-name hadn't sweated about texting the wrong family of criminals in *A Fistful of Dollars*. Simon pressed each letter with the care of a man trying to diffuse a nuclear bomb:

> Hi Sarah, it was just great to meet you properly this morning. I can't believe we haven't spoken at Badminton. I'm very competitive and I mus ...

Simon deleted the part about being competitive, he thought it would make him sound like a jerk who has to be in control. Not a good second impression.

> ... at Badminton. If I'm being honest, I had noticed you lots of times but I always felt a bit shy about talking to you. I always assume beautiful women like you are out of my league.

He knew the bit about noticing her could easily be called in to question and the "beautiful women" line was pure slime, but he so rarely got to be *charming* and he wanted to see how well, in his new-found freedom, he could handle that side of things.

> ... out of my league. I would love to meet for that cup of coffee or maybe dinner? Let me know when you're free and we'll arrange to meet. Simon

He checked and re-checked the name and number and slow-motion pressed Send. *Message Sent* appeared on his mobile screen. He re-read the text twice and slowly began to wince. Oh no, it's wrong, wrong, wrong, he thought. The last sentence was ALL wrong – indecisive and woolly. He should have suggested a time to meet, be more Cary Grant than Hugh Grant, and offered a selection of restaurants. But how was he supposed to think

straight in light of the situation with Meredith. He was spinning in all this confusion – talking to his own hand was a clue to his current emotional psychology. He looked at the palm and the fingers and began to imagine a face looking back at him; the eyes full of disbelief that he had sent any text at all to any woman other than Meredith. He was just a traitor to love now. He picked up his mobile phone and began to compose a follow-up text to Sarah; something to squash any plans they might be about to make. Surely there was supposed to be a period of mourning over the Meredith scene? He wasn't supposed to just leap in to bed with the first attractive, intelligent and sweet woman he spoke to – was he? No, definitely not.

He worked through the horrors of a potential follow-up message: I can understand why you might think it odd that I would lie about that woman I play badminton with not being my girlfriend when she is in fact my fiancée – although technically she's *not* a girlfriend anymore. She *was* a fiancée and now she's, we ... it's a break of sorts, a cooling-off period...

Message received was displayed at the top of his mobile screen – *Sarah*

Dinner sounds lovely. Tomorrow? S

All fear and about the whys and wherefores in seeing Sarah dropped away like old skin. The reply to Sarah had to be just right; not too keen and needy, and not too aloof and *whatevah!* Simon made a cup of tea and ate three jaffa cakes, sat down to think and began to emote with care: Great! Fab! He stopped, ate another cake and started again. Did anyone, in their right mind – perhaps a children's television presenter – actually say *fab* anymore?:

Dinner tomorrow sounds lovely.

Simon had been told before the importance of parroting

certain keywords back at people if he wanted to impress them, and *lovely* was a word he liked to use whenever possible – like *horrid,* although people always seemed to laugh at that one.

We could meet in town, outside the town hall perhaps, at eight o'clock? I'll book us a table at Morrigan's, if that's okay with you? Si

He pressed Send, watched the envelope fly across the screen and disappear and then sat back and waited. He closed his eyes and thought about the last thing he had said to Meredith: ' ... time to deal with this ... process the anger ...'

A reply landed with the *Message Received* sound he always enjoyed:

Great, Si, I'll see you there and then. Sa xx

She had put two kisses on the end of her text. Were they *really* at the kisses stage? She was *already* calling him Si – he hated Si. Why had he signed his last text Si – had he just forgotten the 'M'? Was she *really* asking him to refer to her as Sa? How would he even start about pronouncing that: Sar? Sair? Za?

Why hadn't he considered the possibilities of his text; the open invitation to interpret his words and shorten his name in anyway seen fit? And was he supposed to begin their romantic evening with a synopsis of his life, a likes and dislikes list (including his huge dislike of Si) followed by attentive listening and one eye on the door; waiting for Meredith to walk in with that Ian-guy or some other body from Marketing and PR?

The restaurant was the place *they* always went; it was where the waiters knew their faces. And the two of them took every opportunity to fake any celebration – just to validate the money spent; enjoy the delicious shortcrust pastry pies with the range of forty different fillings. And he hadn't even bothered to find out

whether or not Sa(rah) was a vegetarian or vegan or fruitarian.

Should he just cancel the date? It *was* a date. How could he have a date now? He had only just walked out on Meredith. He was in shock, confused by the door of opportunity opening. But surely he couldn't go on a *date*? It wasn't a gentle chat with a friend. It was a loaded evening of sexual tension and of introductions – to a new life, new interests and potentially a new body in his bed. He hadn't been intimate with anyone else for years. And how would his body look to a new pair of eyes. Would he look pasty and out of shape? Was he supposed to have a six-pack? And, worst of all, would he ejaculate too quickly? He made a promise to himself to never say the word *ejaculate* out loud. It was all assuming she wanted him in her bed and didn't make some excuse about getting up early in the morning. How was he supposed to know when to make a move on her? He would need to take advice from Sean – without the hysterical self-questioning.

He asked himself a few last questions: Was it wrong to process the anger with a nice supper and good company? Was it so awful to deal with his pain by talking to someone over candlelight? And was it really that bad to be taking Sarah to his and Meredith's favourite restaurant?

Chapter 7...

He woke up as Sean turned his front door key and walked in.

'Hallo?' Sean said. He looked around the side of the lounge door and smiled. 'So ... who is this woman? No, no, wait a sec. Let me get settled.'

Sean went to the kitchen and brought back two bottles of beer.

Simon gave his friend the lowdown on the morning. Sean winced and grinned in all the right places and Simon found himself enjoying the agony and the ecstasy of this new-life, post-Deangate, place he found himself positioned in. He revelled in the telling of his run-in with Meredith. Who, but a scumbag, could take any dramatic pleasure in such an acute situation?

He told Sean about his parting shot; the curtains being drawn as he waited at the bus stop and then meeting Sarah, and the horror of blurting out "mating". Was he really this nasty? Did he have no soul? What about Meredith – he had to make sure she was all right; he would call her later. Had he, in fact, been waiting all these years to move in with his best friend and become Chandler and Joey from *Friends*?

'Jeez, your life is beginning to sound like Morrissey lyrics,' Sean said. He sat back and swigged the last of his beer. He breathed out heavily and shook his head. 'Pizza?'

'Maybe later, yeah, actually pizza sounds awesome,' Simon said. He had a memory flash of ordering what he thought was a deep-pan uber-pepperoni pizza in Florence, with Meredith, and ending up being served a thin and crispy frisbee-like meal covered with assorted colours of peppers. Meredith had thought it was hilarious – he hadn't. But he had laughed anyway.

'Let's get the order in now. There's that local place and they hand-make them, but they do take ages to arrive,' Sean said. He pulled his iPhone out and found the number. 'What's your pizza poison? It's on me.'

'Deep-pan pepperoni, cheers. No peppers.'

Sean placed the order and went to the kitchen; bringing back another two bottles of beer.

'So, my guru of women, what are my options?' Simon asked Sean. They both sipped the beer and sat in thoughtful – or faux-thoughtful – silence for a few seconds.

'Well, contrary to everything anyone who knows me would usually say or think about my ability to empathise I'm genuinely conflicted, my padawan.'

'Thanks for that, Master Yoda, but I don't have the Force to fall back on and I really can't be bothered to think up any lightsaber jokes right now.'

'Anxious you are,' Sean said, in his best, vaguely approximating, Yoda voice. He smiled, leaned forward and carried on – minus the *Star Wars* references and impersonations. 'No, really I am. I mean on the surface of things it seems obvious that you have the absolute right to seek sexual compensation for what Merry did to you. But ... '

'But what?'

'But, is that *you*? I mean, it's definitely *me* and I would be right out there looking for a revenge shag. But you and Merry are my best friends and you *are* good together. And I do mean good. She is so right for you. She doesn't take any bullshit but she allows you to be yourself, indulge some of your more adolescent pursuits, such as your friendship with me. And true, yes, she is a little overbearing at times and pushy and ...'

'I get the picture, amigo,' Simon said. They smiled at each other and drank more of the beer.

'My point is that this *isn't* about just sex, which is probably what she and this Dean guy were about.'

'I don't want to think about that.'

'No you don't, but you have to. Sex is nothing, well not *nothing*, but it's usually just two bodies pressing and bumping and hoping something will make them forget any existential pain, the hopelessness of their lives ending with certain death. This is *your* life, this thing with Merry and it's real and good. It's your whole future. I know she's fucked things up, but that was in the past. She's done it and it's done. Don't do a Tony Blair in Iraq and get dragged along on the back of dodgy, inconclusive evidence. Be smart and ask yourself questions about how you want this scenario to end.'

'So, what *are* my options? I like what you're saying and, almost unbelievably, it makes sense, but I can't, just can't, go back there and say, Ah well, these things happen. C'est la vie, etcetera.'

'Okay. I see it like this, and I've been thinking about this today. You could see this as a chance to have your own six month sex-fling, just like Merry did with that De ... oops, sorry. And you could sleep around while keeping things ticking over with Merry; go to couples therapy, long walks in the park, deep and meaningful chats, that kind of thing. Or you could cancel your date with this other woman, what's her name?'

'Sarah Marshall.'

'Like the Russell Brand film?'

'Not like that in the flesh, only the name.'

'She looks like Russell Brand? Yikes.' Sean laughed. Simon swiped his beer bottle towards his friend and pulled a face of derision. 'Sorry. Right, so she *doesn't* look like Kristen Bell? That's a bummer, man.'

'Not really. But come on, tell me more.'

Grease was one of Sean's favourite childhood films and he couldn't resist the opportunity. 'Tell me more, tell me more, was it love at first sight?' he sang.

'No, and she didn't put up a fight either, Kenickie. Just give me the rub.' Simon was amused but beginning to become frustrated; sometimes Sean took the digression-conversations between them just *too* far. But Simon was impressed with the more serious tone his friend had found to describe which way he might head for in the rest of his life.

'Well, you could start serious separation proceedings with Merry, go the whole hog and break up with her permanently. I don't think anyone would blame you for that. To be completely

honest, I'm not sure this Sarah Brand Kristen Marshall lady will be the next *one* in your life. She's rebound material even if she seems great right now. You're still raw as hell about this. She's a temporary fix, but the fact of the matter is that you have this opportunity. It's a painful thing, but it's a chance to start over; move on to the next part of your life. You are young, good looking and intelligent, a great catch for any lucky lady.'

Sean sat back and sighed. He sipped more beer and had the look of a man who has exhausted himself with giving good advice – satisfied but tired with it. Simon leaned back too – the bamboo frame of the sofa digging in to his back. Stupid cheap furniture, he thought.

'The only problem with all of this, all these decisions and options, is that I still love Merry so much,' Simon said. He sipped beer too. He felt silly talking about love in such a sentimental fashion; as if he should know by now that it wasn't enough just to love.

Sean nodded knowingly.

'Her dad said I was a saint for forgiving her the ... indiscre ... thing with that other guy, that mudder fugger. Fucking Simon-saintly-fucking-Templar, yeah, that's me, folks.'

'Ah man, that *is* a name you got there. The way your dad stitched you up. It still amazes me you two are so close. Most people, when they realised the telly connection, would have made plans to leave home, never to return.'

'Yeah well, I was about five or six when I twigged to the name comparison, not really the ideal age for thinking about flying away. It's one of those time-taking-the sting-away things. I mean, who the hell knows about *The Saint* these days anyway? Apart from telly geeks and Seventies revivalists. That awful Val Kilmer film version of the story killed any future *Saint* stuff. And thanks be for that.'

'So, what's it gonna be?' Sean asked.

'Another beer sounds mighty, mighty good to me,' Simon answered. He held up his bottle and smiled.

'Good answer. But I was actually referring to your predicament about tomorrow and the rest of your life. To date or not to date, that is the question?'

'The pizza's here.' Simon opened the front door, found a couple of pound coins for a tip and took the two hot boxes back to the lounge. Sean had brought more beer through.

'Let me mull over things while we eat, drink and watch *Swingers*,' Simon said. He opened the boxes, passed Sean his pizza and sat back to enjoy the film. They had seen it many times together and apart – it had become an icon in their friendship; a symbol of the knowing crassness in young male behaviour; an exaggerated gift to all the *lads* who think they're in control of various scenes with women. A sobering, cautionary tale which Sean and Simon adored – both of them assuming a position of knowing better than the characters how and why and where and when to *be* a decent guy; but both secretly feeling as if they were constantly bordering on the same ridiculous male clichés.

The film ended. Simon felt a bit drunk but didn't want to make a fool of himself. It had been a long day, full of incident and unresolved situations.

'That film just gets better and better. Although I always feel a bit sad that Vince Vaughn and Jon Favreau haven't made anything as good since. I mean, *Dodgeball* and *Iron Man*, give me a break. And the fact that both of them have gotten so fat,' Sean said. He yawned loudly and stretched. 'Any decisions made, amigo mine?'

Simon snapped out of his daydream. He had been thinking about Meredith's smile, specifically a week ago as they lay next to each other after sex on a Saturday morning. They had eaten croissants in bed and read *The Guardian* and Meredith had

smiled for such a long time as they listed possible honeymoon destinations. But she wasn't smiling anymore. Simon still felt as if he didn't really know anything about the Dean-phase. He hadn't been ready to hear anything from Meredith that might sound like an excuse. But he did, at the very least, owe her a day in love-court. She had the basic right to explain herself to him. If she wanted to.

'I think so. I am going to meet Sarah Marshall tomorrow, have dinner and take all of that really slowly. And I'm going to work on things with Merry at the same time, you know, talk it through, find out why she did what she did.'

Sean nodded. He twisted and turned his mouth and looked uncomfortable.

'What's up?' Simon asked.

'Well, to be quite honest, that was the option I was *least* hoping you'd take.'

'Because?'

'Because I think it will probably backfire and if you do get back together with Merry there's always the chance, a very strong chance, that you'll look like a dick when you bump in to this Sarah lady. It's a gauntlet you're going to run, but that's the spice of this life, eh?'

Simon felt unsteady in his reasoning, as if such an obvious flaw hadn't appeared in his logic. He hated the sense that he might be heading into a void of misery of his own making.

'I've got to feel some sort of ... some kind of reckoning with all of this. I don't like lies and cheating but I do want some emotional justice and balance. I probably won't do anything or get anywhere with Sarah anyway. I've become like *Bagpuss*, a house trained would-be- husband-cat-type, fiercely domesticated. In other words a complete bore to new women.'

'You might be surprised, man,' Sean said. He stood up and

yawned and took the empty beer bottles and pizza boxes to the kitchen. And then came back in to the lounge. 'Right, I'm off to bed. Night dude.'

'Night.'

Chapter 8...

The following day Simon tried to refocus his energy on his job, a virtual impossibility with the Sarah Marshall evening ahead. He received hourly text messages from Sean – who thought he was being hilarious –from nine until twelve o'clock all asking the same question: Forgot Sarah Marshall yet?

And he had an itch-like need to send texts to Meredith. He had a visit from his boss, the area manager, later that day; the only reason he had bothered turning up for work. He had been honest with Marion just after he arrived that morning – filling in as much detail as he wanted her to know about moving out of his house and what had happened with Meredith.

'I've got to say, I'm really shocked at her behaviour. I always liked her. I can't believe she'd betray you like that. Are you certain she actually did it?' Marion said

'Did what, sleep with this other guy for six months while I thought she was with me and only me? *Yeah,* I'm completely certain and sure about that, Maz.' Simon began to regret telling his assistant manager. She was invariably judgemental about other people's issues.

The area manager came and went within a couple of hours after lunch. He picked holes in various parts of the book-shop organisation – window displays, and some very old and

un-returned books which he assumed Simon had forgotten about, which was true.

Simon nodded and apologised and promised better standards. Simon needed this job, but he would love just one chance to tell his boss how useless he thought he was – all the banal statements about trade discounts – *boring* – and which books were missing the relevant money-off stickers – *again boring* – how much time he wasted on the road between bookshops and how little respect his managers had for him, that much was true.

He also made endless inappropriate sexual comments about female members of staff to Simon, which Simon found repulsive – he had picked his team carefully and genuinely liked them. After the sexual comments and shop-based negativity, the repugnant area manager would inevitably compound the horror of being associated with him by unleashing his laugh, which was more of a fast-paced snuffle.

But the absolute reason for Simon's enmity towards him was his insistence on humming the opening bars to the theme tune from *The Saint* as they walked around the bookshop.

***

The day finally over, Simon caught the train home and texted his father from the carriage:

> Hey dad, how are you? Don't know whether you and mum know yet, Meredith and I are on a break – we're taking some time away from each other. If you need to call me, then call my mobile. Ciao. Xx
>
> A text was fired back from his father very quickly:
>
> Simon, what is going on? Mark called us last night. He sounded

very upset. He said Meredith isn't talking to him and that you've moved out. Mum and I are very worried about you. What's happening? Dad xxx

Simon set his jaw and ran his tongue around the inside of his mouth in annoyance. Mark knew exactly what was going on, it was his fault. Well, not *all* his fault, but the delivery of the revelation – and the concomitant level of fallout – was completely his fault. Simon looked out of the train window and sighed. What was he supposed to tell his parents? That he was a fool who had placed his trust in a cheater? They loved Meredith and if they found out the truth and Simon did find a way to forgive and forget, the relationship between his parents and his future wife would always be *difficult* at best. Perhaps Mark had been wise to keep quiet about the reasons for the separation. Simon began a reply to his father:

Wedding jitters, dad. Nothing to worry about too much. It's me being a donkey-brain about getting married – bit early I know. Mark and Merry aren't too happy, but Merry wants me to be sure, so I'm living with Sean for a while. Don't worry. Love to you and mum xx

Jeepers, Simon. It sounds a bit odd, but okay. If you and Meredith are all right then so be it. Call us soon. We love you, son. Dad xxxx

Simon smiled and deleted the text. He began to write a text to Mark:

Just texted my parents saying I've got wedding jitters and am living away for a while. It's best for them to believe the 'fault' is mine until things sorted out. Don't worry, Mark. I don't hold you responsible for any of this. I'm just sorry it's happening. Simon

A reply pinged back:

Thanks, Saint. I'm so bloody sorry I blurted that out. I feel like such an old fool. I AM an old fool, a drunken one at that. ATB, Mark.

Then Simon knew he had to text Meredith – or should he call her? No, she would still be at work and he had to get his mind in to the right shape for his evening out. He started writing, she hadn't replied to his incomplete text the previous day:

Merry, hi. How are you? I've been texting my dad and yours and, for now, I'm taking the heat about us not living together. I've told my parents I've got wedding nerves and need some time to get my head straight – not a complete lie of course. How are you? I'd like to talk again. I hate the way we left things, this whole situation sucks and I want you to have a chance to tell me why things went the way they did. Let me know when you're free next and I could come over or we could meet in town ... Sim

He thought for a moment or two or three and wondered whether he should or shouldn't put any kisses at the end of the text. Sarah had put some at the end of hers and she hardly knew him. And weren't kisses just a friendly sign-off anyway; a way of saying cheers, like/love you, have a good one, a bientot?

He added two kisses – a bench mark of care; one would be too business-like and perfunctory, potentially sounding a sour note and three would be too cloying and needy. He sent the text and looked out of the train carriage window again. He received a message almost instantly; opened it and realised it was from Sarah:

Still on for tonight? Sa xxx

She was Sa again, a real live person. He had used all his

grounded, so-called, charm to win a date with her and he had to keep going with that mature-lover performance now. One of the great things he knew and appreciated about a long-term relationship was the easing down of the fakery involved in courtship/dating/ making moves/getting it on. He enjoyed the easing down part the most and had completely forgotten the stress levels in the forming of romantic alliances. He had found Jane Austen frustrating to read as a child – his mother was the National vice-chair of the Jane Austen Society in Bath – and whether his summer holidays had been truncated with *Emma* or *Pride and Prejudice* he had always ended the books feeling exhausted by the twists and turns of each of the characters attempts to find love. He had once asked his mother why it took them all so long to get to the point; why couldn't they just ask each other out for a drink. She had told him that manners in "those days" wouldn't allow that sort of behaviour, and that, in any case, they didn't have television or the radio and didn't have a lot else to do.

He hadn't really given any more thought to her shortened name – was he still Si to her? – and how he might have to incorporate it in to conversation. Fortunately most people in an intimate setting didn't usually use each other's names. Were they intimate yet, when did that begin? And she had used three kisses! Cloying and needy? Or sweet and caring?

Surely it was better to *know* she was on his side before the evening began and that she had a positive attitude to the whole thing? He knew he was just full of nerves. All he had to do was relax. He had the whole thing under control and there was always Sean to fall back on for advice.

He should text Sean now:

Mate, quick advice time. Just texted Merry re: meet-up for chat etc. Sarah Marshall texted just now for a confirm on meet-up

tonight. She used three kisses and called herself Sa again. Do I use three kisses too and do I keep on with being called Si?

Sean replied within a couple of minutes:

Merry meet-up good idea. Three kisses before first date?! WTF?! Only use one kiss in reply. And if you want a few (potential) weeks/months being called Si, as in: 'Touch me there, Si, oh, yeah, Si ...' etc then keep it up (bad pun, sorry). Personally, I would switch sign-off to Sim or Simon ASAP. Later, dude. Text me. Call me. Love me!

Simon was smiling when he received a reply from Meredith, but the smile didn't last long:

Heat about us?! What are you talking about, Simon? If you want to break up with me, be a man and DO IT! I want you to move your stuff out for as long as you're away from the house and from (evil) me. If you want to meet and talk that's fine. I will be around most evenings, but call or text first. I think you're being a bit ridiculous and immature – all this back and forth, but if you need to revert to being a teenager to sort yourself out then good for you. M

No kisses from Meredith – no business-like marker, no care, no cloy: just a basic *fuck-you*. He read the text five times before he deleted it. He was about to arrive home.

He got off the train. But not before getting his head caught in the separating doors. Some pushy fool behind him doubled-pressed the open/close button and poor Simon, who was doing a final read-through of Meredith's scathing text, was not concentrating on the momentum of the departing flow. He winced as the thick rubber border of the doors bumped against his ears and cheeks. He tried to pull his head away to no avail and took a confused moment, when the doors finally withdrew, to gather himself and realise what had happened. No one apologised to him or tried to help. He hadn't registered who had pressed the button.

Life's just *too* good sometimes, he thought, as he walked away. He smiled grimly at his own irony, rubbing his hot ears and running fingertips across his cheekbones, and began a text to Sean:

Just got head squashed getting off the buggering train, some git closed doors on my head! People are just bastards, eh? Anyway, Merry texted me back and told me to get my shit out of the house asap and called me a teenager in a man's clothing. Said I was making everything worse and indulging myself. Am I doing that? Any ideas on a reply, amigo? I want to be The Thomas Crown Affair cool about this – the Pierce Brosnan version as opposed to the Steve McQueen one, always thought McQueen's was over-hyped. Help!

Simon stopped by a flower stand and thought of buying a bunch for Sarah. Too much? He was about to ask for lilies and then stopped himself. He always bought lilies for Meredith – she liked the midst-of-life-we-are-in-death aspect of their reputation and called them *serene*.

'White roses, please,' he said to the stand assistant. He couldn't bring himself to buy red roses. If he did that, he may as well turn up at the restaurant with a box of heart-shaped chocolates too and maybe wearing nylon, ankle-flapping trousers. He always associated man-made fibres with losers.

A text arrived from Sean:

Fuckus me, my main man! That sheet is baaad from Merry. What is she going on about, what have you done to deserve that? Did you tell her about the evening ahead, does she know about Sarah

Marshall? My advice is do the Tommy Crown Affair thang and don't text her back right away. Hold the frustration, hold the anger and w ... a ...i ...t. C u later, maybe?!

Simon texted right back:

No! to her knowing about Sarah, that would be Armageddon – and I don't mean the Bruce Willis film. I told her I was taking the rap for moving out for a bit from my folks. Both of my parents are bugging out about the split and I don't want them to know full-time result yet when it's only half-time (does that even make any sense?!) Merry went batshit about the idea that there was anything to feel bad about and then laid me out with the adolescent accusation shite. Nice, eh? Later.

From Sean in reply:

That is some egregious crapola. As I said, DO NOT REPLY YET. Ciao.

Chapter 9...

Simon took the flowers and caught a taxi home. He didn't want to wear his work clothes for the evening out – a tweed jacket, loose fitting white shirt and flowery tie. He had worn corduroy trousers too and been told by Marion that he looked like a university professor. The area manager thought the joke was hilarious and this only reinforced what Simon already knew: he was extremely disliked by his boss. Marion's shoulders shook as she laughed at him and the area manager snuffled laughter out as if he was about to stop breathing – Simon had smiled along – what else could he do, he wanted to karate-chop their throats; secretly despising them.

Simon showered quickly, styled his hair using too much wax, with the finished effect reminding him of a Victoria sponge cake. He gripped the sides, pushed the fringe up, down and forwards. Nothing helped. It looked like a disaster – a cake-shaped disaster. What did a Battenberg look like? Was it postmodern and ironic enough to get away with?

He could only imagine how Sarah would spend the whole evening trying to avert her eyes from his head. He would not and could not allow his first date in years to be ruined by the shape of his cakey coiffure – inappropriate drunken comments and overwhelming use of film metaphors might always wreck his romantic encounters, now and in the future, but not a hairdo. He washed his hair again; forgetting the conditioner and opted for some of Sean's hair gel instead this time. It didn't look much better – a bit like the lead-singer of early 1980s synth-pop band, A Flock of Seagulls: wings up at the sides and a ski-slope of a fringe. He closed his eyes and tried to think positively.

'But you have such a *nice* face,' Meredith's mother had told him once as they sat sipping Pimms in her palatial back garden. He had been considering a goatee beard and she had been telling him what a bad idea it was.

'*Nice* face. I have a *nice* face,' he said to himself. 'Is that the same as when someone says you have an "interesting" face? Because we all know what that means don't we, huh, huh? That means El Freako ugly-bug should-be-in-the-circus face. Great.'

Simon caught a bus to the town centre, walked to Morrigan's and found Sarah waiting outside. He had had a tacit plan to arrive early; place himself facing the entrance and, in the manner of Cary Grant stand slowly and walk to Sarah as if *he* was the restaurant

owner – the image he wanted to convey was: Man of the World, Mr Casual-Lover (with a hint of sophistication).

But she was already there. She looked very beautiful – he had forgotten much of her looks from the previous day; his mind was so full of Meredith that Sarah had become a reflection of that, but she was very different. She had put her hair up at the back and wore a wide diamante clip to keep it in place.

As they walked into the restaurant the waiter greeted them – a waiter Simon had seen many times but discreet enough to ignore any recognition – and took their coats. As Sarah sat Simon noticed she was wearing a small, black formal evening dress. He remembered his mother telling him, as an embarrassed teenager who did not want to hear such things from his mother, about the effort women go to when they really like a man. And that men never seem to notice or bother to make the same kind of effort in return. And now Simon felt like a complete scruff and wished he had tried to break the trend.

He had stayed with the corduroy trousers, tweed jacket and only changed his shirt – he hadn't even shaved. And then, of course, there was the hair. He smiled and listened to Sarah's small talk about her day at work – she worked in an architect's office. Simon was nodding and smiling, but was unable to stop the nerves in his stomach about Meredith walking in, and thinking all the time that his hair might be expanding vertically – and that he would eventually catch sight of himself, in the back of a spoon perhaps, only to realise that his bouffant-ish, frightwiggy mop looked exactly like an 17th century French aristocrat.

'So how was your day? What is it you do again?' Sarah asked Simon.

He had to take a moment to think about what he did actually *do* at work. He could tell her about his constant checking in with Sean about the date – she might like that, but then again, she might just think he was a loser and walk away before they had even broken bread. He could talk evenly and in detail about book returns, discounting since the ending of the Net Book Agreement and the lack of a kiss on the end of Meredith's text, but that was *maybe* for the second date chat.

'I manage a bookshop, it's very dull. Most people who work in bookshops think it's something a bit special, you know, an intellectual backdrop to feed the masses great words, but it's just retail,' he replied smiling and realised quickly that self-deprecation wasn't quite the same thing as self-laceration. Sean would be cringing if he were here, Simon thought, women hate the self-pitying guy. He wasn't usually self-pitying, he was usually too happy and feeling too lucky in life to pity his lot. Was this how he would be forever, in the wake of Merry's confession? It was a horrible thought.

'That sounds very interesting actually, I love books. What's your favourite?'

'*Young Hearts Crying*. It's by Richard Yates,' Simon said. He was relieved he could think of a great author to name. He did love the book and had read it four or five times. Meredith had more forgiving tastes than him and was willing to read most genres. She laughed at Simon's elitism. He told her life was too short to read "rubbish". And she always told him that variety was indeed the spice of life.

'Oh yes, the guy who wrote *Revolutionary Road*?'

'Yeah that's right. He was a terrific writer, had a terrible life, though. Alcoholism, manic episodes and rejection. Suffered like all great artists should, I guess. What's your favourite?'

Sarah laughed and Simon felt a surge of power.

'*Green Eggs and Ham*. I love the silly sense of Doctor Seuss.'

Simon nodded and wondered if he should try and match the quirky answer – what could he offer? John Grisham wasn't quirky.

Neither was Donna Tartt. He had started *Humboldt's Gift* once, but Bellow wasn't quirky at all. Doctor Seuss was a great answer, even namechecked in an R.E.M song once.

'Did you see the film version of *Revolutionary Road*?' Sarah asked.

'Yes, I ...'

The waiter returned and took their orders. Sarah chose a vegetarian pie and Simon ordered a steak and kidney. He wondered if his choice had been a bad one. He started presuming Sarah would see him as a blood-sucking murderer of baby cows. Was he truly ready for that kind of observation from another woman other than Meredith? Surely he deserved, in the getting-to-know-you stages, a pass on value judgements?

He had been living, albeit happily, with the constant evaluation of his actions and reactions for years and he wanted – even in the headbuzz of what had happened in the past couple of days – space to just be himself. Then he stopped his mind in its tracks and realised he hadn't finished his answer about the film and that Sarah hadn't blinked or made any facial indication that she disapproved of his food order. They ordered a bottle of red wine too, which soon arrived. The waiter poured them both a drink and as he walked away Simon raised his glass, clinking Sarah's in mid-air. He drank slowly and looked across the restaurant at the table he and Meredith had sat at last time they visited.

'I did see the film, *Revolutionary Road* that is, and I thought it was great. I wasn't too sure about re-teaming Leonardo Di Caprio and Kate Winslet after *Titanic*, which I hated ...'

'Really, you hated it?' Sarah interrupted him.

'Yeah, absolutely. Didn't you?' Simon was incredulous. Surely everyone secretly hated that film. James Cameron messed up important historical details and created a mass-market, dumbed-down blockbuster from a tragic event. *And* he had employed Celine Dion to sing.

'I thought it was a lovely story, and I thought Leo and Kate were great together. Really lovely.'

Simon had always had a problem stopping his passion for his own opinion overwhelming conversations. He wanted to burst in to a full-scale discussion about the great early works of James Cameron – *The Terminator* and *Terminator 2, Aliens* and *The Abyss* – and the crass commercialism of his recent-ish output – *Titanic* and *Avatar.* But he managed to stop himself. He would save that for Sean.

'Fair enough, but *Revolutionary Road* was the real deal, eh?' Simon wasn't sure he knew what the *real deal* meant in this context and as he drank more of the wine – glancing at Sarah, who was biting her top lip – he knew she had no idea either.

The food arrived shortly after and broke the silence. They both made noises about how good it all looked. Simon ordered more of the wine.

'Delicious wine, isn't it? I don't know anything about countries, vintage or vines, but it tastes fantastic,' he said without thinking; knowing he sounded like a fool. He ate quickly and punctuated mouthfuls with more and more wine. Eventually he needed to visit the toilet. He excused himself and stood up. The restaurant was virtually full now and Simon could feel himself involuntarily swaying towards the toilets. Other diners looked at him – some smiled knowingly, some shook their heads. He smiled and tried to remain steady. After he had flushed the loo, he looked at his reflection in the over-lit mirror. His hair seemed to have found a way to mimic the hideous look of a wind-tunnel victim; standing up and sticking out in all directions. He thought he looked like a court-jester: his cheeks were alight with the booze-buzz and his eyes were looking bloodshot. Thank god for candlelight, he

thought, trying to use some water to flatten and rearrange the style.

He returned to the table, making a great show of walking calmly and in a straight line. He thought later that he must have looked so obviously drunk – like the driver caught by the police, over the limit, making every effort to prove his sobriety. Sarah smiled at him, but the smile was that of the worried companion – the one who is considering what to do and how to deal with the problems of the other person. Simon sat down and felt a need for honesty wash over him.

'Sarah. I need to be honest ... by the way, before that, on your texts you sign off S A – how would you pronounce that?'

Sarah looked puzzled. 'Erm, I'm not really sure, no one calls me that,' she said.

'But surely someone *must* have called you that if you use it in your texts?'

'No, not really. It's just a short-ish and more personal way of signing.'

'Ah, okay.' Simon poured himself more wine and offered more to Sarah who shook her head.

'What did you want to be honest about?' Sarah asked him.

'Yes, honesty is good. Good stuff, too.'

Simon had now reached the point of being so drunk, he was only aware of what he had said after a two or three second time delay – a post-babble horror story was emerging. He was becoming completely unlikeable. His inner-Simon was screaming for it to stop to be beamed away by Scotty, back to the *Enterprise* – maybe Bones McCoy or Spock could help him re-energise his common sense...

'So, what do you want to be so honest with me about, Simon. *I* have to be *honest* here, I'm beginning to feel uncomfortable,' Sarah said. She shuffled slightly and the side of her left eye twitched in such a way that Simon imagined she might cry.

'Nah, no, I mean. I just feel, am feeling, a little drunk about... this. Not about this thing we're doing. I feel a bit sad about how things are ...'

He stopped and sipped some water. Jeepers Jesus and Mary, he thought, what am I talking about anyway? Was his mouth attempting to re-locate itself on his face and, in doing so, just spilling out loose talk about everything and nothing? He quickly glanced over his shoulder to see if a police SWAT team was waiting in the restaurant doorway for him to overstep the line of common decency and render all rational explanations for his behaviour defunct. A bullet to his head might solve the tricky lips problem.

'Simon, please. What is it you're trying to say?'

'Okay, that's only frar, I mean fair. I am single now. Sort of. But I wasn't *that* single when we met.'

'What does that even mean? You mean you're going out with someone?'

Sarah's face had become a picture of anguish; a picture that Banksy might have displayed on a wall in London, a send-up of Saint Sebastian, covered in arrows. Sarah was looking at him as if all hope had been drained from her by some restaurant-dwelling leech, who enjoyed the low-light ambience and the torture of first-date women before the later seduction of their men; a succubus who would later turn on Simon and, post-demonic coitus, sit on his bed with a cigarette and argue the relative merits of James Cameron's foresight in *Avatar*, and the way he created a new wave of cinema and the re-emergence of 3-D.

'It means Meredith and I ...'

'Who is Meredith?'

'My girl ... my fiancée, well sort of not now, but we're on a break, you know, like Ross and Rachel were in *Friends*, and ...'

Sarah began to stand up. She beckoned the waiter, who arrived quickly. 'May we have the bill, please.'

'But ...' the waiter began to speak.

'The bill, *now, please*,' Sarah said, through gritted teeth.

The waiter nodded and walked away.

'This is total shit, Simon. I'm guessing that Meredith *is* the lady you play badminton with? And that you've fallen out with her and fancied getting your end away with some silly cow like me, eh? That's just lovely. You're a real prince, aren't you? You tosser.'

Simon blinked a few times, sipped more wine and thought of Prince and his tongue, the naked Prince on his album cover *Lovesexy* – and then he thought about Dean, and then Meredith, and then Dean again.

The scene, Sarah looking over his head for the return of the waiter, and then glaring at him as he forked more pie in to his mouth; each time followed by more wine, felt too surreal to be true. And Simon's fuddled mind began to retreat into a Happy Place – he mentally curled in to a foetal ball and thought of good times.

Eventually the waiter came back. He laid the bill in front of Simon. Sarah snatched it up, grumbling, 'Sexist.' She took a twenty-pound note from her purse and placed the bill and money back on the table.

'Well, mister badminton bastard. Have a good evening and a nice wife, oh, I'm sorry, I mean life. Fuck you very much.' And then she pushed past him and walked out.

'Sarah, I like you. This wasn't meant to be a bad deal. I just wanted to disclose the true stuff and not be a git about ...'

But she was gone, he was shouting and he was being watched by other diners.

Simon rubbed his eyebrows and finished his food. He looked at the bill. There was still twenty-five pounds to pay, but, for the sense of calm after the storm of crushing emotional defeat, he would have gladly paid five times that amount. Simon pulled out his mobile phone and began a text to Sean:

Hey man, forgetting Sarah Marshall won't be a problem. She just roasted my nuts, wigged out on me and left. Am pissed and pissed off. Any advice?

A reply came back quickly:

OMG. WTF? What did you do, vomit, Mr. Creosote-Meaning of Life stylee in her soup?

Simon smiled, thinking of the film reference, and wondered if he should have tried that Monty Python approach instead of the so-called honesty: No.

Worse than that. I was honest about Merry. I told her all about the break and the relationship stuff. As I indicated previously, I am p i s s e d!?

Sean responded:

What?! Why, why, why? I know Sarah M was only ever going to be a passing thang, but you could, at the very least, have seen her a few times and, maybe, just maybe, have seen her naked a few times too. Oh, mate. I am sorry the shit has hit the fan – thinking of the literal shit from that scene in Airplane! Any chance you can stop her, text her, sober up, lie a little?

Simon placed a ten and twenty-pound note on the bill tray and handed it to the waiter, who had just cleared the plates. He poured the last of the wine; watching the final red droplet ping the surface of his quarter-full glass:

I really don't think it's likely that Sarah M will ever forgive this evening. I was really, well, really knob-ish. Only way I can think

of to describe it, will tell you more later, about my way with the words. I'm trying to think of a good movie comparison, but it's still too soon to be definitive about that. Shit hitting fan will do for now. And I am in front of the fan! On my way home v.soon. Ciao.

Chapter 10...

Simon flopped in to Sean's house an hour after his last text.

'So your life is officially a Todd Solondz film now, eh?' Sean said. He looked around the lounge door and smiled at Simon.

'Yep. I am an additional character in *Happiness*, similar in nature to Philip Seymour Hoffman's guy, but without his odious charisma, or perhaps with it.' Simon sat on the sofa opposite his friend and they grinned at each other. And then they burst in to laughter.

Beer?' Sean stood up and walked towards the kitchen

'No thanks, I've had enough, just water, please.'

Sean brought the drinks back and sat to listen. 'So, my son, I am ready to hear your confession,' Sean said. He held his bottle of beer between his hands as if in prayer.

'I royally fucked up tonight with Sarah Marshall. I think I *can* forget her now, and am beginning to feel as if my chances at regaining happiness are slipping away.'

'What are you seeking to achieve?'

'I don't have a clue at the moment. Any thoughts? I don't want to let time just get away from me on this. I think I'm going to see Merry as soon as poss and get the making up done. I want my old life back. I'm clearly crap at new relationships and all that jazz and I have a chance to repair the best thing in my messed-up life. Yeah?'

Sean sucked air and breathed out hard.

'So that's a no then? Come on, come on. What do you think?'

Sean shook his head and bit his bottom lip. 'Man, you know what, this is all *totally* fubar. I want you to be happy and if going back to Merry makes you feel that buzzy good stuff inside then great, do it. But to be completely, and uncharacteristically, honest I think it's a mistake to be doing it now. She has fucked you over and dissed you big time about the post-confession fall-out.'

'True enough. But she's upset about ...'

'She's upset?! She's the one who fucked this Dean guy for six months. Six mothering months! *You* have the right to feel upset. She has the right to feel a few other things, such as: annoyance at her dad for blabbing, humiliation for a lie caught. But *upset* with you is not on the agenda. Personally, having thought about it, and you won't like this, I think you should move in here for as long as it takes to start over with someone new and clean break it with Merry.'

'So, that's what you truly believe? Wow, okay.'

Now Simon breathed out hard. He sat back and sipped some water. 'Thing is, it's all unfinished business in my head and I have to do more than just walk off in to the sunset. There are always hanging-on feelings. I know what you're saying makes sense. Hell, if I was in your shoes I'd be saying the same shit to you. I'm going to text Merry this evening and go around to see her as soon as I can.'

'And if she keeps up the arrogant stance about this?'

'Hopefully she won't.'

'Your life, amigo. I'm off to bed.' Sean stood, took his beer bottle to the kitchen and left Simon with a pat on the shoulder as he walked out of the lounge.

Simon took out his mobile phone and began to compose a text to Meredith:

> Hi, just wanted to find out how you are and ask to see you asap. I want to talk about all of this, a proper conversation, not an argument. No recriminations, I promise. I miss you. I miss us. When is good with you? Sim xxxx

He placed his phone on the table next to the sofa and re-filled his glass with water. There was a message-received beep as he walked back to the lounge:

> Tomorrow, late afternoon if you like. You know what time I get home from work. M

No kiss again. *More fuck-you.* He thought about Sean's words. Was he about to make the biggest mistake of his life, handing a complete relationship-forgiveness pardon to Meredith and, ultimately, giving her the power in their life together? Would that mean he was a now and future cuckold? A coward? But he didn't want to face endless evenings like this one. He texted Meredith back:

> Good. Okay then, tomorrow. See you then. Sim

He stopped his natural inclination to add some kisses after his name. He didn't want to offend her, but fuck-you was a two-way street.

Chapter 11...

The following day Simon found himself sleepwalking through his job even more so than the previous day. He thought of texting Sarah Marshall, trying to mollify her with apologies, explanations and the hope of a recovered date. But he just couldn't summon any real urgency, she was a lost cause. The only urgency he truly felt was the one which made him convince Marion that he needed to leave early; rushing home to buy lilies for Meredith and getting his hair cut before he caught a bus back to his house. He was determined his hair would never ruin a social situation again – a double-crown didn't help his attempts at persuading the top of his style to lie flat, and there was always a hint of fly-away, flip-top hair.

He had wanted to be waiting for Meredith outside the front door, casually leaning on the low garden wall, flowers in hand and looking *dashing* – that was her word for the way he looked sometimes. He liked it too, it always summoned images of old movie stars to his mind.

Simon waited and waited. It was already nearly an hour later than Meredith usually arrived home. Simon puffed his cheeks out and considered himself punished – that she was deliberately finding things to faff about with at work as another fuck-you to him: a test of sorts; like the recruits waiting outisde Tyler Durden's house in *Fight Club* wanting to join 'Project Mayhem'. He felt more like the pathetic Meatloaf character from the film version than any of the cool-suedeheads in the club. He texted Meredith and walked down the road to buy a fizzy drink and a newspaper:

> Hi there, am waiting (and waiting) for you to get back. You did say you would be back at roughly the same time as usual. That was nearly an hour ago. Any ideas on ETA? Sim

He was about to walk in to the newsagents on the corner when a reply came back:

Bugger. Completely forgot you were coming over. Should be back fairly soon. M

This was the biggest fuck-you yet. The big mama of diss – no sorry, no rushing back immediately. He bought the paper, left the drink, and wandered up the road to the local cafe. She would have to wait for him now. He ordered a pot of tea and some toast and sat down to text Sean:

Unbelievable. And no, not the ravey early 1990s single from EMF. Merry has put me down biiig time. She has deliberately kept me waiting for over an hour, and then when I text her, she's all like, oh well never mind, I forgot, it's only you, blah, blah ... I know, I know, you told me not to do this, oh wise friend.

Sean fired one back, from the hip:

Get the hell outta there! Leave her a note on the door, maybe something cryptic to make her think twice about pulling this shit again, maybe pin a chicken's head to the note too. She's got the upper hand; any chance at resolution for you, with you in control is slipping away. Go, Johnny, go, go, go ... You're unbelievable – boom!

Simon slurped his tea and replied:

Again, I know you're right. You are right. But I'm here and she's coming back right now. I have to see this through, even if it means we argue and break up for good. I'm full of readiness for the kill – or some such crap.

Sean responded shortly:

Fine. Your choice, bro. Here when you need me.

Simon smiled at the text and finished his food and drink. He tried to avoid looking at his watch. He desperately wanted to be *cool* about things. Meredith would have home comforts to wait with. But eventually his nerves overtook his reason and he couldn't wait any longer. He left the newspaper on the cafe table and darted back down the road, trying not to run. The lilies were beginning to droop and he began to hate them – their deathly connotation was like a chant, and was drowning out his babbling thought stream.

He dumped them in a bin on the corner of his street and took a deep breath. His heart was thumping and his face was burning. He slowed his pace, noticing Meredith's car parked outside the house. Sunset had passed and the streetlights were on. He enjoyed the darkness acting as his cover as he approached the house. He didn't want her to feel any further advantage on this occasion and see him coming up the pathway to the front door.

He stopped by the low front wall again and looked through the front window. He remembered, many times, as he was drawing the curtains from the other side of that same window, feeling a sense of unease that he really couldn't have seen anyone looking in from the outside. But now he had *that* advantage. He expected to see Meredith any moment; perhaps changed from her work clothes, maybe holding a cup of tea. And then he saw her. And then he saw **him**. A *him* he didn't recognise. The man with Meredith was about the same height as Simon; had short brown hair, in a messed-up-just-out-of-bed style, and he was about the same age as Simon and Meredith. He was wearing a suit. Simon's first lateral thought, after a few seconds of: Whhaat, whaata fucki, fuckkka?! became: *Dean.* That <u>must</u> be Dean. She is waiting to confront me with Dean, he thought, to end things in a James Caan being shot to death in *The Godfather* metaphorical fashion.

Simon ducked away from the window. Now his upper torso was covered in cold sweats. He felt glued to the spot and knew he had to force his body away from the house as quickly as possible.

'Oh. My. God,' he said quietly. 'This isn't real. La, la, la, la, hey, hey, kiss him goodbye,' Simon found himself singing Bananarama and wondering, for a moment to distract himself from the onset of trauma, whether Dave Stewart and Siobhan Fahey were still married or not.

'Eurythmical bananas,' he said out loud.

He found himself hopping, skipping, tripping and whipping his head left and right; looking back over his shoulder to see if Meredith and the presumed-Dean were following him – or perhaps now having sex against the window. Dean might have his tongue out; flapping on the window pane, waiting for Simon's imminent arrival and decimation.

He crossed the main road and began to wait at the bus stop, but this was where he had met Sarah Marshall the other day and he simply could not risk seeing her, especially in these moments of horrific self-analysis; a close-up on the burning of a soul. He wanted to find a tree too and empty his bladder.

He ran along the pavement to the next stop on the bus route. But that still wasn't far enough away, so he went on to the next and the next – eventually coming to a breathless stop. His mobile phone beeped and buzzed in his jacket breast pocket. He knew it would probably be Meredith wondering when he was going to arrive, or maybe Sean trying to draw him back into the land of make-believe relationships/friendships, where the lines of decency, morality and tongue girth are drawn tightly and people can live in oblivious happiness and pretend the Deans of the world don't exist. He ignored the phone and jumped on the next bus.

Chapter 12...

Simon walked from the bus stop back to Sean's house – the wind in his hair and a sense that there was no way *Home*. Simon walked up to Sean's front door and realised *he* had the power of time and silence and that he could live in a new fashion now – any old way he fancied.

'So?' Sean said, as Simon slumped on to the sofa.

'Buckwheats. Buckwheats.'

Sean's eyes widened. This was part of their adopted film code; certain terms and phrases from classic films summed up a moment or a feeling so perfectly that it was all that was required. Buckwheats was stolen wholesale from *Things to Do in Denver When You're Dead*. And Buckwheats meant the most painful way to be murdered – such as a shotgun being fired while inserted in your anus ...

'The irony that Garcia played Jimmy The *Saint*, and you ...'

'Yeah, *great* irony. I know how he felt at the end now.'

'So what went down?'

'Meredith on Dean most likely.'

'What? Last I heard you were waiting for a basic face to face.'

'Okay. All right. Let's set the scene. I walked from the cafe on the corner, darkness all around.'

'Thank you, Philip Marlowe,' Sean smiled. He hurried to the kitchen and brought back two bottles of beer. They clinked a cheers and Simon sat back to continue.

'I wandered towards the house, thinking, "Why rush this? She made me wait. Now she can wait too". I felt pretty good. Bit of a swagger in my step, almost a Gene Kelly in *Singin' in the Rain* mood. And then I saw her in the lounge, through the front window.

And then I saw him, some guy in a suit and it was Dean. And then the Buckwheats began.'

'Woah, woah. How do you know it was Dean? Was he wearing a t-shirt saying: Bad Guy Dean in the Lady of the House?'

'No, obviously not. But who else could it have been? And, even if it wasn't Dean, it was some *other* guy. Some *other* guy with her in my house. They were close together.'

'I'll admit it does have the ring of a Buckwheats deal. She knew you were about to arrive and you wanted, deserved, a private audience; and yet she chose to have some interloper there, which is mega-provocative. But maybe you should have confronted that shit, man. Maybe you should go back or call her now and tell her what you saw and how it made you feel. Why should you be the only one to suffer the whole Buckwheats shebang?'

'I'll text her later ... or not. I just want to get lost, like Chet Baker, without his fall from the window and the death. Just out of this *fug*. Can we go out and pull some really nasty ladies and party with them?'

'Fugging hell. I'm sorry, what did you say?' Sean said. He put his hand to his ear, as if he had not heard Simon properly; a smile formed on his mouth; a knowing smile, followed by one raised eyebrow. 'Did you just ask me to unleash my true self? You want to rock this party?' Sean sang the question.

'We want to rock this party,' Simon replied.

'Let's fly like those Conchords, baby,' Sean said. 'But first we need to change into partay clothing.'

They were both changed and ready to leave within fifteen minutes. Simon switched his mobile phone to silent – ignoring the buzz of the incoming call; knowing it must be Meredith.

'Was that Merry calling?' Sean asked Simon as they walked to the train station.

'It was. It is, every ten minutes or so.'

'Should you at least text her to say you're not coming over?' Sean asked, stopping in front of the ticket machine.

'Fine, fine. If it makes *you* feel better, I'll do it now.' Simon smiled and took his phone out.

'Oh yeah, this is all about me, hmm, yeah,' Sean said, smiling and stroking his chin.

Simon opened the messages from Meredith. He fully expected to be affronted by more of her annoyance, but the words were full of worry: Where are you? I'm beginning to panic. M ... Are you okay? Please call me to let me know you're all right. M

And the voice messages sounded concerned about his health and welfare too, although they began with a slightly withering tone of disbelief that he hadn't been waiting for her, and the sluggish post-work tiredness she always seemed to feel these days – he assumed she was tired on this day because of all the Big Dean lovin' she'd been through.

He got on the train with Sean, nodded at his phone and pulled a face of expectancy and dialled Meredith. She answered quickly.

'Simon, where are you? Are you all right? Why didn't you come over? What's going on?'

He breathed out, faked a toothy smile to Sean and tried to think where he should begin his reply. Simplicity is best, he thought.

'I'm on a train with Sean. I'm fine and I *did* come over. I waited and waited, as I said in my text to you earlier. I went to the cafe around the corner, the one you've always hated because of the greasy film on the tea, and I waited some more. And then, when I had finished my grease-filled tea I walked back to the house to see you. But instead, I saw something other than just you. What do you think that was?'

'What? What are you talking about? I thought you wanted to meet and talk about this. Now you're sounding like a Raymond Carver short story. I know I'm the one who screwed up, but ...'

'No, no, no. This is one step beyond screwing up. I. Saw. You. I saw you with that suity-guy in the window. And you know what, I don't want to hear any excuses about who he was or wasn't. I don't really care.' Simon waited for a moment. 'I want to call it a day. It might seem too quick to make that call, but this is killing me slowly. I keep picturing you with that mother-of-fuckers Dean guy. I don't want to talk anymore now. I'll arrange to collect my stuff soon, maybe through your dad, and we can talk about the house and the rest some other time.'

'But Sim, this *is* too quick. Don't make a rash decision. That guy you saw in the window wasn't any ...'

'Enough!' Simon shouted. Sean looked shocked and a few other passengers glanced at Simon. 'Enough already. I don't care who he was. I've already said that. I've got to go now. So, goodbye.'

'I love ...' Meredith tried to say the best of heartfelt final words, but Simon closed the connection.

Simon put his phone in his pocket and looked at Sean.

'Do you want to go ...'

'Just give me a minute,' Simon said and stood up. He walked to the nearest toilet, closed the cubicle door, and sat on the grey plastic seat which was covered in cigarette burns. He put his face in his hands, covering his mouth and silently screamed. He had blown his life away – Simon wondered how *he* ever could recover from this.

He realised the train was about to come into the central station, so he stood, looked in the mirror – his face seemed a combination of different colours: red cheeks, green-ish lines under his eyes and his forehead a clammy white. He hoped it was a false impression. This *was* supposed to be a party-night and he wondered what lovely woman would find him attractive if he seemed to be transmogrifying into Kermit the Frog. He prayed the facial effect was a product of the harsh on-board lighting; he felt better knowing he could still be this vain even in the moment of emotional collapse.

Chapter 13...

Sean was waiting for him by the exit doors and looking anxious. They jumped off seconds before the train departed.

'Shall we kick off with a quick drink and chat here?' Sean asked.

'Sure. Mine's a large whiskey, please.'

Sean went to the bar and ordered two whiskies; as he waited he glanced back at Simon – smiling and nodding. Simon gave him a thumbs-up to acknowledge the care and concern. They sat and drank in silence for a while; listening to the sound of high-speed trains rushing through the station.

'So what did Merry have to say for herself about the mysterious character in the window? Was it Dean?' Sean said.

'She said it wasn't anyone in particular. I didn't want to hear the bullshit drawn out in to some kind of self-justifying soliloquy, so I talked straight through her explanations. It's all crappy crapola of the crappest kind. I saw what I saw.'

'Well yeah, but what if she was telling the truth? I mean it could have been someone coming over to collect an Ebay purchase or a colleague from work?'

'It's a lie. She is a liar. Why are you sticking up for her?'

'Well, to be honest, and you *know* I am in your corner over this issue, the Dean-affair thing and the rest, but she hasn't had your full attention yet. You're blinded by anger and hurt, and that's completely understandable, but I reckon, as you've started down the road of hearing her side of things you should finish it.

Otherwise you'll never know what happened, yeah?'

Simon swigged the last of his whiskey down; held up the glass to indicate he wanted another, waited for a moment and then Sean nodded too.

Simon walked to the bar, the bitter burn of the whiskey made his tongue dance about in his mouth – tongues again he thought, closing his eyes briefly before ordering the second round. He paid for the drinks and also bought a tin of *Cafe Creme* slim cigars and a box of matches. The last time he had had a cigar was two years ago at a barbecue. Meredith had been out at a hen night; he and Sean had been invited to a mutual friend's meat feast. The evening had been a red wine and Champagne frenzy, punctuated by undercooked chicken and sausages. There had been a moment – Simon could vividly remember the *feeling* in that moment – when the combination of the booze, raw meat and cigar had bound tightly in his gut and he had stopped mid-sentence and rushed to the nearest toilet, spending the next ninety minutes wishing to die.

Sean hadn't suffered at all; instead laughing at him the following day, saying that perhaps the problem had been the origin of the cigars – the fact that they were advertised as Cuban, and yet *Produce of the EU* was printed on the side of the packet.

'Really? Life in hands time again, eh?' Sean said as Simon offered him a cigar. He took one and leaned forward to share in the lit match. 'Actually we can't smoke these in here,' Sean said, pulling back and putting the cigar in his breast pocket.

'Fuck it,' Simon said. He took one drag and put the cigar out; holding the smoke in his cheeks. He knew Meredith would hate the thought of him smoking anything – he was mildly asthmatic.

'Say Scotty, what's it gonna be?' Simon sang to Sean.

'A gin and tonic sounds mighty, mighty good to me.'

'I wonder whether that band had any real success after *Swingers* came out, that was such a cool song,' Simon said. The whiskey had fortified his determination to have a good evening with his best friend.

'Big Bad Voodoo Daddy? Who knows. That's the kind of question the internet was built to answer. Shall we go?' Sean said. He stood up, Simon followed, feeling a bit wobbly from the hard liquor.

'Where to?' Simon asked as the evening air hit him.

'There's a kitsch-cool night at Jamestown. Fancy that?'

'I live for all things kitsch and cool, you know that.'

Sean grinned at him and winked.

They laughed and walked off, firing lines from *Swingers* at each other until they reached the club venue. There was a queue growing along the side of the building. They joined the end and lit the cigars. Simon felt a zip of thrill down his spine as he looked at the other clubbers. These were his sort of people – not his type for friends, but people he could feel safe around, in keeping with and part of the potential to enjoy himself. They took clothes and hair seriously – something he had let slide a bit in recent years, although he still tried to keep some style in his looks and had been fanatically self-conscious as a teenager, even going through a thankfully short-lived phase of shaving the ends of his eyebrows off because he thought they were too long.

These people around him were determined to have a good time without the need to just get drunk and roll around on the pavement fighting a stranger later. He and Meredith had been to one of the kitsch-cool nights a year or so before, but they felt out of place as a couple among what seemed like single people trying to get laid. And Simon had found himself looking at other women that night – feeling a hefty aftermath of guilt in the following days. He thought about that and considered the cruel irony of his mindfuck moments in light of the Dean revelation.

'Hey,' Sean whispered loudly near Simon's ear. 'Those two over there, very hot and definitely having a *look* over here a minute ago.'

Simon looked at his friend and then followed his gaze to two young women a few feet in front of them – they were both medium height, clothed in flowery dresses with sleeveless arms. They were slim, one with brown hair and one with red, and they both looked *good* to Simon – if only he could ditch the guilt factor; looking not touching was okay, but what if *they* wanted to touch? Would touching through clothing be considered cheating? If the lights were off later and he *thought* he was with Meredith, would that be on the Right side of morality? They were nearing the club entrance.

'Okay. That's a nice start,' Simon said. 'What should we do, offer them a drink as soon as we get in?' Simon began to feel fourteen again – and for him, that age didn't have a particularly positive memory when it came to parties or clubs. He had felt permanently *about* to succeed, although never quite able to move away from the wall in the party room and throw some winning shapes, always on the edge of jumping in with girls and booze at fourteen and then again at fifteen – but no. And then at sixteen, in the haze of spliff smoke, he had finally lost his virginity to an eighteen year old called Faith Dugwood. Now he was thrown back into old feelings of 'how" and "when" with new women in dark rooms with coloured lights and big music.

'Well yeah, we could do that, but we could also relax and see who else is in tonight?'

Simon raised his eyebrows and nodded. He would defer to Sean in all things single on this night.

They walked into the club and paid the cloakroom attendant. Sean found them a table and bought drinks – vodka and tonics. The interior had changed a great deal since Simon's last visit;

there was now a stage and a microphone, plush dark-red curtains as a backdrop. He guessed there might be a band later, or perhaps a comedian. The tables were circular and small, three chairs to each one – more floor space to cover. And there were leather-seated booths around the large room, but they were all taken – one of them was partially filled with the two women Sean had noticed outside. Dean Martin was singing *Volare,* one of Simon's favourites, but a nasty reminder of *that* name. And the scene made Simon feel as if he was about to see a Rat Pack show from the Sixties: Sammy Davis Jr hamming it up wildly, Sinatra smiling and tipping his trilby, while Dean Martin made a joke about wearing glasses – because it left his hands free to pour more booze ... bah da boom!

'So, have you seen who's over there in the booth protecting some space for the *right* guys?' Simon said, sipping his drink and leaning towards Sean.

'Of course, already given them my winning nod.'

'Winning nod? What is your winning nod, some sort of horse-like communication tool?'

'Yeah, right, just like that. And next I'm going to rear up and snort a hello at them, offer a hoof. You've got to be cool, this takes some finesse.'

'Okay. All right. I'll buy in to that. The only thing is, if we sit here being all coy and noddy and finessing it, won't that just leave the door open for some other smooth operators to move in and grab our spot in their booth?' Simon was enjoying the chat and the chase. He felt an excitement in his stomach; a good-times buzz like the ones he had felt every time he had seen Meredith in the first few months of their relationship. For their first date they had played things safe and gone to see a film – *The Bourne Identity.* Simon had particularly wanted to see the film because it had been directed by Doug Liman, who

also directed *Swingers*. And he particularly wanted to see it with Meredith because, after reading many pre-release reviews, he thought it would send the right message to her about his credentials as both a man who liked action, but also a man who liked intelligence and life with a cohesive plotline. What a crock of a plotline his life was now. If only *he* could "pull a Bourne" and lose his memories.

'If that happens, it happens. They aren't the only lovelies in here tonight. The place is filling up with them, look around,' Sean said. He smiled at Simon and nodded over his shoulder.

'Ah, master, the nod of expectation and foresight, I think,' Simon said. He laughed and allowed himself to be guided by Sean's lead, glancing around the room – which seemed even grander now, more like a hall of mirrors and lights, with orange flood-beams and a glitter ball that sparkled above them. Simon's eyes followed the spin of the ball and he soon realised he was close to being drunk; a recent memory-recall made him think of running down a street with his zip down and his dignity on raw display. He decided his next drink would be a soft one.

Some people had started to dance and a swing band had set up on the stage. Simon wondered where they had come from.

'You know what, amigo,' Sean said. 'Let's make a move on the booth bunnies now and if that *doesn't* work out we can always make changes later. Yeah?'

'Sure thing, daddio,' Simon said. His stomach dropped as he stood up with Sean. He finished his drink, left the glass on the table and then felt as if he didn't really know what to do with his hands as he walked to the booth. Maybe he could have a secretive chat with his old friend-hand and ask it to keep mum if things became steamy later.

'By the by, in the same way Trent and Mikey slightly distorted the truth in *Swingers* regarding what they did for a living, my suggestion is we do something similar. I mean, this is a one-night thing, yeah?' Sean said.

'Okay. What do you do? I want to be a writer. I'm a novelist, working on a new book about ... well something I'll come up with later,' Simon said. He felt better at the thought that by pretending to be someone else, he might by twisted psychological extension *not* be cheating on Meredith. He wasn't a real-life Simon Templar anymore. He was a version of the television character – a persona the series might have used.

'That's good. But remember to be convincing about the details, women listen to the details, stay sharp on that. I'm going to be the singer in a swing-revival band, the next revival that is.'

'So not the Nineties revival? The next revival that no one actually knows about yet?'

'Yes, *that* one. The one *I'm* reviving!' Sean laughed and slapped Simon on the back. They arrived at the booth.

'Good evening, ladies, may we buy you some Champagne and perhaps join you?' Sean said. The band were striking up behind them; beginning with *Cherry Pink and Apple Blossom White.*

The two young women looked at each other and then smiled at the young men in front of them.

Simon let Sean make their introductions.

'I'm Sean and this is Simon. And you are?'

'I'm Lorraine and this is Nikki.'

Simon thought to himself: Lorraine – red hair. Nikki – brown hair. Remember the hair code when too drunk to put a name to a face.

'Would you like some Champagne?' Simon said. He looked at Lorraine and not sure why but he liked the shape of her eyes, very round and bright. He made sure he looked at Nikki too.

'Lovely, may I have a strawberry in mine, please, thanks,' Nikki said.

'But of course you may. I'll help you with those,' Sean said, raising his eyebrows and nodding to the bar.

'So, the brows *and* the nod this time? Are we going to compare performances, expectations and overall modes of communication like that all evening?' Simon said, smiling and zinging a friendly fist-bump off Sean's jacketed shoulder.

'Let's just get a quick settlement deal sorted before we go back. Are you cool with trying out for Lorraine and I'll go for Nikki?' Sean said and leaned on the bar, ordering four glasses of Champagne. The band was now playing *It happened in Monterey*.

'Cool. That's a perfect fit for me. Although I'm feeling so weird about all of this. I mean, it was only a couple of days ago that my life seemed ...'

'We're here now. This is a one-nighter, not a party for the Four Horsemen. Let's go with this. And as Bobby De Niro said in *The Deer Hunter*, 'This is this'. This *is* this. Yeah?'

'Right. Okay. But didn't things go really badly for him and his buddies in that film...'

'Yeah, but anyway. The point is, we are here and now and we both know this could be a very cool evening. Focus. Focus on Lorraine. Dance away your fears, amigo.'

They collected two glasses each and walked back to the booth. They sat back down and passed the Champagne around, all clinking glasses and slipping into conversation about jobs and music and films. Simon was surprised at the ease he found in his mouth and the flow of chatter he managed. Sarah Marshall slipped into his thoughts a couple of times, but he managed to elbow her to the sidelines and listen intently to Lorraine. Simon glanced across the table at Sean, who sat very close to Nikki. He had his arm around the back of the booth and was deliberately leaning very close to her mouth as he listened. Ah, a true professional at work, Simon thought.

'Would you excuse me a moment,' Simon said to Lorraine eventually. He had been trying to persuade his bladder that it wasn't that full for about twenty minutes, but he had now reached the stage where his legs were crossing and uncrossing every minute or two and he just *had* to go. He smiled at Lorraine, then at Sean and Nikki.

'Can I offer anyone a refill on my way back?' Simon said.

'I think four more sounds good,' Sean said.

Simon saluted him and walked off.

Chapter 14...

Inside the cubicle Simon had to stifle the urge to bark out a groan of satisfaction at the relief he felt. He was drunk now and found himself having to squint at the toilet bowl and zone in on the exact range and angle he was taking. Finally finished, he zipped up – he wouldn't suffer the run and flap indignity again this soon – and opened the cubicle door. As he washed his hands he looked at the mirror in front of him. There were two men standing behind him, *watching* him.

'Evening gents,' Simon said, immediately wondering what had possessed him to say *anything* at all.

'Evening matey, having a nice time with your pal and the ladies, eh?' one of the mirror men replied. They were both tall and well-built, one more so than the other. They weren't dressed for kitsch either. They looked like lager-boys in any city on any Friday/Saturday night.

'Er, yes. Everything okay here?' Simon said. He felt a flush of anxiety erupt in his cheeks and a keen sense of jump-back-in-to-

the-cubicle enter his head. And he wished Sean was there with him.

'So, this is what we need from you, it's very simple and I know you had no idea you were pissing on the wrong bonfire this evening. Make your excuses to Lorraine and Nikki and leave. Leave now and we'll all be friends. Okay with that, matey?' The larger of the two men said the words and looked over Simon's shoulder, pushing his short hair about a bit and re-styling it to look exactly the same way.

'Right. I'm guessing you're their boyfriends?' Simon was too drunk to stop *some* words coming out of his mouth. The scene seemed too odd for him not to make a comment or ask a question. The alcohol was slowing his common sense.

'Something like that. Anyway that's not your problem *is* it?' the smaller man said. He had dead brown eyes. A look in his face that told Simon, even in his drunken, hazy state of twisting realities, stop talking and start walking.

'No, true is that, and that it is true. I will put it to my men.' Simon had meant to be amusing, quoting Michael Caine's German officer in *The Eagle has Landed*. But he instantly knew the film reference was a bit esoteric, and no one was laughing in its wake.

'You laughing at me, wanker?' dead eyes said. He stepped towards Simon.

'Chillax, Chris, chill,' the larger one said, putting his hand on dead eyes shoulder. 'Just get your mate and fuck off out ... and that would be *now*, okay?' the larger one said to Simon, staring into his eyes in a way that made Simon quite certain that if they had to continue "convincing" him of the validity in their arguments they might use the inside of the toilet bowl as a tool of persuasion.

'I'll talk to him, sure.'

Simon moved away from the wash-hand basins and back in

to the sparkle of the club; as if he had re-entered a cool, musical Narnia.

He felt the vibration of his mobile phone in his jacket pocket. He looked at the bar, thought of the Champagne; looked across the tables and through the dancers to Sean, Lorraine and Nikki and wondered what he should attend to first. He pulled the phone out and read the message; fully expecting it to be words of hurt and anger from Meredith. But it was from Judy:

> WTF is going on in your head? Merry's a complete basket case. She's staying with me and she won't stop crying. Can you tell me what you've said or done to her? I can't get any sense out of her and I think I'm at least owed an explanation ... Judy x

One kiss. Business-like, but no fuck-you. That was Judy all over. Simon looked over his shoulder but couldn't see the toilet thugs. But he knew they'd be watching his moves. Would sending a text be a breach of his forced promise to them to leave? Would any delay mean he was cruising for a bruising? He began to type a quick reply to Judy:

> Listen, you'll need to get some explanation from Merry. Not me. I'm not willing to go in to this horror story. Suffice to say, and I need to say this very carefully: I AM NOT TO BLAME FOR THIS. That statement is paramount. I love Merry, that's all important too. Thanks for being with her. I was worried how she'd cope. I'll call you soon. Text me whenever you like. Sim xx

He sent the message and looked around the room again for the terrible two; again no sign. Were they hiding? A figment of his drunken imagination? And then he spotted them near the entrance, mostly in darkness, and they were watching him. He smiled and nodded, but wanted to flip them the bird and poke his tongue out at them. He walked back to the booth and forced a

smile at Sean, who was now sitting between Lorraine and Nikki with an arm slung over each of their shoulders.

'Mate! No Champagne?' Sean pronounced the last part of the drink: *pania* 'What gives? The girls and I are thirsty and we were thinking of having a dance after that. *You* like to dance, don't you?'

Sean was waggling his eyebrows and nodding to each of the women – Simon knew he was annoyed at the lack of booze.

'Actually, they're just chilling the bottles. And I really need *you* to help me get the drinks. Can we go to the bar now, please? Right now would be good.' Simon tried to keep his eyebrows under control, in fact he made certain his entire face was still and that the only expression he would betray was slight amusement – he was acting the Playboy, who was so laid back he was happy to wait for his Champagne to be correctly chilled.

'Okay, okay, I'm coming. And then, ladies, when we return let's drink and dance, eh?'

'Sure thing,' Lorraine said. She smiled at Simon and he felt a pang of weakness in his limbs. All he wanted in that moment was the chance to take Lorraine home and see what a new body felt like to his senses.

Simon's mobile vibrated again. He pulled it out quickly – a quick read-through now and he would respond later; unless it was life or death. Judy again:

> Jesus, Simon, again WTF? What does all of that mean? Just text me and tell me what the deal is? I love you both but I'm dealing with a devastated Merry here and now. So ... J x

'So, why did you take so long in the toilet and start going on about chilled bottles? It doesn't give the greatest impression of being the Guy behind *the* Guy, in the shadows, man of mystery and all of that good stuff,' Sean said. He placed a comforting hand on Simon's shoulder as they stood at the bar.

'I was ... talked to in the toilets, about the girls and about leaving,' Simon said. He looked at the spot where the lager boys had been standing – they had moved on.

'Talked to? By who?'

'A pair of goons. Two guys who looked a bit like they would happily watch us both burn, maybe having a laugh at us as they poured petrol into our boxer shorts. They were just over there.' Simon nodded over his shoulder.

'What the hell? And what did they actually want, you said something about the girls, and us leaving?' Sean looked around the club. He looked at the booth, Simon did too, Lorraine and Nikki smiled and waved at them. They both waved back. Simon smiled at Sean.

'They said *they* were with the girls and that we should leave immediately or suffer the shit.'

'What? This is ridiculous. Listen, let's find these twonks and talk them down. They probably spotted the girls outside too and they're looking to use some muscle to take our places. And you know what? They can just fuck right off. Yeah?'

'Well yeah, fair enough, but I really can't be bothered to fight about this. I mean, we've only just met the girls and, personally, I haven't been in a fight, a proper fight, since I was about thirteen, and then I got stabbed in the leg with a pair of sewing scissors. This is beginning to feel like Ross and Chandler getting bullied in that episode of *Friends*, the one where ...'

'Yeah, yeah. Is that the guys, over there, by the stage?' Sean said; he flicked a nod stagewards.

Simon looked around. The toilet-two were right there, by the stage, the band bouncing around behind them. They were both glaring in Simon's direction.

'That's them, yeah. Let's just take the drinks to the girls, make our apologies and head off, okay?' Simon said. He felt a throb in

his head; as if the heat had been turned to maximum in the room and as if he was in the mid-stages of spontaneous combustion. His mobile phone vibrated next to his chest again. He pulled it out and read the message:

> Saint, Mark here, what is going on between you and Merry? Probably none of my beeswax, especially considering my verbal blunderings, but I care deeply what happens to you both. If you have time, please contact me. TTFN. Mark

'No, no, no. We're going to go over to their table; offer them a drink each and ask them how we can resolve this. But first we need to attend to the ladies. They need Champagne. You take their drinks and meet me by the brainless brigade table. Yeah?'

'Sean, come on. Listen, you and I both know how this shit will end. I've got enough to deal with at the moment. I've already had the Sarah Marshall horror. I really don't want to do this.'

'I'm *not* going to just walk away from this. Those girls are lovely and they clearly like us both. Let's just sort this out, that's all. There's no need to worry. Guys like that are full of shit; all talk. Come *on*.'

Simon was always reluctant to admit flaws in his best friend, but the character trait of sheer *belligerence* was too amplified in Sean's nature to be ignored. And once he saw a goal; a purpose – regardless of its futility – he was virtually unstoppable. Simon winced. He wanted to throw his head back with a primal scream. He knew he had the option to walk away, but he was living with Sean now and owed him so much. He had an obligation to play out his role as a wingman, he knew the obligation was a bit immature and ridiculous, but he was Goose to Sean's Maverick. This isn't *Top Gun,* though, he thought, and Goose dies.

Simon collected two Champagne flutes – he left his own drink on the bar, he was too drunk to need more alcohol and his stomach was churning around with nerves – and he walked back to the booth.

His legs felt heavy with anxiety. He avoided looking towards the stage, half-expecting to hear a scuffle beginning. He attempted his best smile and looked directly at Lorraine. She gave him a smile right back that took him by surprise; a smile full of warmth, a genuine smile that made his heart race. He knew in that moment Sean was right; that even if he ended the evening with no teeth and a face folded inwards from the sheer ferocity of a fist pummelling he had *that* smile to keep in his memories for good. Meredith gave him those smiles and a feeling like that most of the time – would he just walk away from her if some thug told him to?

He set the drinks down in front of Lorraine and Nikki. 'Hey, do you know those two guys over there by the stage?' he asked them. Simon moved to one side to allow them a better view. He watched Lorraine's face for recognition. She seemed shocked.

'Is Sean talking to them about us?' she said.

Simon looked around. Sean was sitting with the musclebound pair; he was smiling, and Simon began to relax, imagining the best. And then Sean's hands went up, in a gesture of contrition – as if he was about to be gunned down and was asking for mercy. 'Yes, they think they have a right to your time and attention. They collared me in the gents and told me to get Sean, and then get out. Any ideas who they are?'

Lorraine looked at Nikki. And they lied to Simon and said no. He knew it was a lie. Who looks to someone else for confirmation of an identity? he thought. He half-expected their noses to start extending.

'Right. Okay. I'm just going to have a word with Sean, back in a moment,' Simon said to them and walked away.

Simon joined Sean and interrupted the "difficult" conversation. 'Sorry to butt in, just wanted to say sorry and we'll be going now,'

Simon said to the angry pair. They looked at him as if they wanted to kill him. He smiled and patted Sean's shoulder, lightly pulling his jacket to pass on the tacit message: Let's get the hell out of here!

Sean nodded at the men opposite his chair. They both looked at the booth and then back at Sean and Simon; silent and still and as menacing as snakes about to strike.

'What the fuck is going on?' Simon asked Sean as they walked out of the club. 'Did they clarify things at all?'

Sean turned and waved goodbye to Lorraine and Nikki.

'They did clarify a *lot* of things. I was about to come and get you. Apparently the bigger of the two, unsurprisingly I didn't get their names, is *married* to Lorraine and the other one is Nikki's brother. *Her* boyfriend is serving in Afghanistan *and* is the brother's best friend. Lorraine had told her husband she was going to a birthday party. He didn't trust her; followed the two of them here with the other gimp. I had to talk us out of a beating, the big guy is a policeman and the other one's a ... well, who cares what he is. What a mess. Shall we just go home?'

'Sure. Jesus, what a bugger of an evening. This was just too much. I've been getting texts all evening from Judy and Mark, demanding explanations, and that feels like my *real* life, whereas this shit is just ... surreal stuff. I need time to deal with the Merry deal.'

'Fair enough. It was a bad idea, sorry, man. Let's put the high life on hold for a bit, eh?'

Chapter 15...

They waited in silence at the railway station for a while, both sipping takeaway coffee. The train arrived, they boarded and their carriage bumped and swayed its way home. After a short walk they were back at Sean's house.

Simon noticed the pile of boxes outside the front door before Sean and a wave of nausea forced his thinking to acknowledge the truth about them.

'Oh no, Jesus Christ almighty,' Simon said.

'Wassup, my man?' Sean said. He looked at Simon and then at the front door. 'What's all of that doing there?'

'It's a message from Merry. It's my things. She's dumped my shit here. Goddamn it!'

'Holy moly, that's cold. I didn't see it coming, did you?'

'No and yes, and who knows. I'm trying to focus. This is all draining away from me. I've messed the whole thing up. I should just call Merry right now and clear this up.'

'No, no. Come on. She's trying to freak you out. Things look dire right now, the Sarah Marshall thing, then tonight and now the boxes, but you need time to suss out the truth.'

'What does that even mean?' Simon asked. Sean had opened the front door and the two of them carried the boxes to Simon's bedroom. 'I know the sodding truth, Merry cheated and she's blaming *me* for being annoyed and upset about that.'

'Not that truth. The truth about where you're supposed to go from here, back to Merry and a life compromised by infidelity, or onwards in to a life without safety nets and known unknowns, as Donald Rumsfeld would have it.' Sean grinned at Simon. 'Beer and a movie maybe. What do you think, mate?'

'Cool. *Star Wars: A New Hope* sounds like the right pitch to me. Sound good?'

'Your wish, my main man. You need the Force, you got it.'

Sean went downstairs and Simon looked through the boxes – DVDs, books, photographs ripped in half, and then he found a letter. He began to open it, realised he couldn't face any more dejection on this night and instead placed it back in the top box; closing the lid on it for another day.

Simon took out his mobile phone and began to compose a text to Mark:

Hi Mark, things are in the toilet between Merry and me at the moment. I don't know how things will turn out but I'm taking some time away to consider options. I'll try and keep in touch. Call or text if you need me. Yours, Saint.

And then he texted Judy:

Did you know about the boxes? WTF?! Couldn't you tell me she was planning that? Has Merry told you it's all over between us? Do you know any more about how she's feeling at this point in time? Has Merry told you about Dean? If not, ask her, it'll make your hair curl. Hope you're ok and that she is too.

Judy replied quickly:

Simon, I'm sorry about the cardboard surprise when you got home (from god knows where – shouldn't you be banging down my door trying to sort this out?) this evening. I dropped them for Merry. She did tell me about Dean. I think you and I should meet in the next couple of days and talk about this. What do you think?

Simon sighed and started replying:

Judy, Judy, Judy, the boxes mean sod all to me truthfully, they can be moved back any time and they are just full of junk. But let's be honest, it's a bit dramatic and you might (secretly) agree a bit much when I'm not the one who shagged someone else, eh? As to meeting up, that's fine. How about Edwards in town for coffee at eleven tomorrow? Xxxxxxxxxxxxxxxx

Simon smiled at the excess of kisses. He wondered if Judy would think he was drunk, or just a fool – as she usually did. Judy responded as quickly as he had expected:

That sounds good. See you there. X

Simon and Sean watched their favourite movie then went their separate ways to bed humming John Williams's theme tune.

Chapter 16...

Simon was still humming as he sat in a booth facing the front door of Edwards the following day – having arrived half an hour early to fire up his mind with an espresso. He tried to read a copy of *The Guardian* he had bought at the railway station, but found focusing on any one particular story virtually impossible.

Simon was about to order some more coffee and yawn when he looked up, and realised Judy was about to reach the booth. He sucked back his yawn. Yikerooni, he thought, she looks about ready to kill me, why do *I* keep getting the blame for how Merry feels in this?

'Hi, good morning and welcome to the world,' Simon said, without thinking – tension always made his mouth go verbally-disco, as Meredith always called it. She likened his inability to cohere thoughts into simple sentences when he was feeling

stressed to a dance floor frenzy of limbs with no discernible rhythm involved.

'Hello, Simon, and what was that crap about?'

'What what?'

'What are you *talking* about?' Judy sat down with a flourish, throwing her large handbag to one side, running a hand through her fringe and finally locking eye contact with Simon. 'Never mind, too much caffeine in your bloodstream,' she said.

'And a lack of real spice in my life, eh?'

'Yep. Would you be a sweetie and order me a cappuccino, please?'

'Sure, sweetie. Would you like sweetener, sweetie?' Simon's mind was crying out for him to start making sense.

'No, thanks. And seriously, Simon, get a decaf for yourself, you're really being very odd.'

'Sorry. I'm feeling head-vegged. This Merry business is making me nuts.'

Judy smiled at him and he went to order the drinks.

He brought back the cappuccino for Judy and an orange juice for himself. His heart was pumping like crazy and he felt a line of sweat on his forehead.

'Thanks. So, how are you? How's Sean?'

Simon knew Judy's enquiry about Sean's wellbeing was limited to a formality. They had dated briefly some years before and the fling had ended badly when Judy found out Sean was also becoming *friendly* with one of *her* friends.

'I'm okay ... ish. And Sean's still Sean, you know.'

'Yes, unfortunately I do. Bad luck for him on that. Simon, I just don't know what to say on this. I've been as shocked as anyone, but you must understand Merry's my oldest and dearest friend and I can't abandon her.'

'Fair enough. I certainly don't expect that. Do you have any message from her for me?'

'Such as what?' Judy sipped her coffee and shot Simon a look of curiosity.

'Well, some kind of apology for the appalling way she's been handling things. Like the way she kept me waiting outside the house, the guy who was there with her … the whole screwing some other guy thing maybe?'

Simon realised his voice was becoming higher and higher, and louder. He was whining like a child.

'She doesn't even know I'm here, she wouldn't want me interfering and I don't want to get in the middle …'

'So *what's* the point of this meeting?' Simon said. He was becoming annoyed with what he saw as Judy getting *exactly* in the middle of things *and* interfering.

'To see how *you* are and try to convince you to go home and sort things out. This is a mess, that's undeniable, but there is so much love between the two of you. I would hate to …'

'There is a lot of love. There always was a lot of love. And Merry shagged someone else while professing that same lot of love to me. And now, in the stark light of being caught with her pants down, she's all like, 'He's being so horrid about it. He's not being nice to me.' Well fuck that. Fuck being nice.'

'Jeez, Simon. Please calm down. No one is asking you to be a saint.' Judy stopped and smiled at the *obvious* pun for a moment and Simon couldn't help but return the smile. 'Merry fucked up, big, huge, massive time. But she loves you beyond compare and wants a life with you, marriage, kids, the whole deal. Please think about giving her a second chance, eh?'

'I don't know, maybe, possibly. I need some time to get my head in order first. Please don't tell her a word about this meeting, though. Is she going to be staying at your place for a while?'

'For a bit, why?'

'Just in case I need to go back to the house for anything.'

Judy's lips tightened in tell-tale anxiety, as if a skin-magnet had pulled at her face.

'What?' Simon asked. He sat forward; elbows resting on the table. He sipped his juice and waited.

'The house,' Judy said, she looked in to Simon's face with the pained expression of one who has to deliver the worst kind of message.

'Yes, the house is ... burned to the ground? Built on a site of historic value and the council have placed a compulsory purchase order on it? What about the house, Judy, my sweetener sweetie?' Simon's grin was loose and genuine; the coffee buzz had been re-delivered and made him feel in control of his life again. The surge of blood, adrenaline mixed up with the caffeine in his system, made his muscles tighten and his heart race; he felt, as he smiled into Judy's face, as if he could run a marathon, and that everything would be all right in his life.

'The house is fine. But ... well, Merry decided to change the locks and she's thinking about renting it out while things get sorted, or not, between the two of you. I'm really annoyed with her for not telling you this shit herself. Sorry, Simon.'

Judy's face dropped in to sadness. She reached out to take Simon's hand – he pulled it away and sat back. He tried to imagine walking back to his home, taking his front door key out of his pocket – like any other day – then placing the key in the lock and finding he couldn't get in. And then the front door being opened by a stranger who would ask him what he hell *he* was doing there.

How long would he have had to wait before Meredith told him about the locks and the rental process? He had only read a bit of Kafka – some short stories – but he began to think he was being manipulated by some universal Kafka-esque dynamic; that there was a god of chaos and mischief who wanted to watch and laugh as a mortal man fought to regain his happiness – and in the process of searching eventually lost his identity and his mind too.

'Changed the locks. Changed the *locks*. So, let me ask you, Judy, and I appreciate you may not be able to answer this, but anyhow, here it goes. Can Meredith *afford* the mortgage and the bills on her own?'

'What are you talking about?'

'Well, why should I pay for anything at the house when I don't even have basic access to the place?'

'Simon, come on. I'm sure you can talk about this with Merry and get everything ...'

'Sorted out, yes, yes. But why should I pay another penny?'

'Well, *okay*, let's see. If you don't pay anything more, the house will go in to mortgage default, the bank will take it away from you and you'll lose a lot of money, as well as your base with Merry and any hope of reconciling. Anyway, look, Simon, she's upset. She was feeling abandoned and she ...'

'Everyone keeps saying *how* upset Merry is. Poor, poor Merry. May I just say for the record, she spent months shagging some other guy when we got together, hedging her bets. She lied to me, didn't tell me about it herself, probably wasn't ever going to either. And now, in the light of the truth, she's frozen me out emotionally, and literally locked me out of my home. Why, oh why am I supposed to feel sorry for any of that? And I *haven't* abandoned her. I've tried to talk to her, see her and discuss things and ...' Simon had to stop. Judy was crying and he felt like a scumbag. He knew instantly he was taking his anger out on the wrong person.

'I'm sorry, Judy. You've been lovely about all of this. You don't need any of this grief, and you certainly don't need me shouting.'

Simon handed Judy a tissue and touched her hand. 'I just can't believe it, any of it, it's all completely fubar ... fucked up beyond recognition ... *Saving Private Ryan*?' Judy looked mystified. 'For

now I'm done. It's all come so quickly and to be honest I *may* look back and wince at the lack of thought I invested in my decisions at this time but I need to stop the flow of hell into my life. I'm staying with Sean for the foreseeable future and I'll be sending one last text to Merry. I won't mention the house thing, I promise.'

Judy smiled at him. Her eyes were red and wet.

'I'd better go. I said I wouldn't be out that long,' she said. She stood up, wiped her eyes again and kissed Simon on the cheek.

Chapter 17...

Simon watched Judy leave; she was unsteady. Her shoulders moved up and down and he guessed her tears were coming quicker now. He wondered why *he* hadn't cried yet – surely he was owed that indulgence, the expression of loss and frustration he *did* feel deeply – and he guessed anger and its energy were keeping that "pleasure" back for another time.

He texted Sean:

> Not gonna believe the shit Judy just dropped on my head. Merry's changed the locks on our house – my house too! – and she's thinking about renting it out, to strangers – obviously. Managed to be a dick and make Judy cry with my anger about the house, so well done me, eh?! If it's ok with you, I think I may be staying at your place for quite a while. I think this is the continuing of a beautiful friendship – to (mis) quote Bogart. Oh, and Judy still hates your ass!

Simon ordered another espresso and waited for Sean's reply. It came as he burned his lips on the first swig:

Man alive! Changed. The. Locks. Huh?!

Sean and Simon always punctuated the *really* serious sentences in their texts with single word breakdowns – although they usually considered *serious* to be something along the lines of someone defending Jar-Jar Binks's recurring character in the second *Star Wars* Trilogy, or someone else perhaps arguing the case for remaking classic movies, such as the frame-by-frame *Psycho* version from 1998.

Sean's text continued:

For real? Obvs it's up to u what you do now – and of course u can stay for as long as u like; stay for evah! – but I would SERIOUSLY consider your future together. It appears she's doing a LOT of thinking – for you both! Any ideas on your future (together)? Are u still in Edwards? Of all the gin joints ... Bogart coming atcha! Ah, Judy, what a love she was and is, kinda miss her ... Laters.

Simon downed the last drops of his espresso, running his tongue around the inside of the small mug; suddenly recoiling as a clear image of a faceless Dean moving towards Meredith with his snake-head tongue flicking came crashing into Simon's mind.

Simon took out his mobile; he was ready to let fly with a love-ending message the equivalent of a texted nuclear missile. He thought for a few moments about the composition of the text. He thought about what he had said to Judy about looking back in the future and wincing at his idiocy and lack of follow-through in these initial periods of separation. Should he slam the door on the entire relationship and come over as the spurned lover driven mad with jealousy; cutting the heart out of their life together and holding it up to the sun – like an Aztec sacrifice for better times to come? Probably not, although the passion in that idea seemed

very attractive. Another mental image popped in to his head at this point – him as a ripped six-pack stomach Aztec, holding the beating heart of the still faceless Dean up high towards the gods. Simon the warrior, reclaiming his land and woman! He smiled and nodded, and then tried to recall what he had been thinking before the visions of ritual sacrifice and unfeasible physique.

Simon decided sobriety; clinically precise words of feeling was the way to go. He thought of Billy Joel jigging about to the lyrics of his song, *Tell Her About It*: " ... tell her everything you feel ..." But what the hell did Billy Joel know about anything – marrying his uptown girl and getting dumped. Piano playing buffoon!

He began the text:

> Meredith, I hope you're doing ok. I've texted your dad and tried to make him feel less like crap about all of this. He was drunk when he told me about that other guy, and none of this is his fault. I think you need to forgive him, but that's for you to decide. I'm staying at Sean's for a while longer. I think we should probably talk at some point about 'things' between us – house, the future, etc – let me know if you want to meet. To be honest I thought dumping the boxes was a bit OTT. I was going to collect some things soon and the house is still half mine ...

He thought it wise to declare his obvious stake in their property to raise the idea of its future – rented out or not – without compromising Judy.

> ... I'll be brutally honest, Merry, I can't (at this time) see any way forward for us. You've been fairly stubborn about the ramifications of all this mess. And it isn't a mess I caused ...

Simon paused here, knowing that blaming her over and over to her (texted) face was guaranteed to make matters a lot worse.

... although I haven't been great at the objectivity thing either. So, I hope you're all right, where ever you are. I still care hugely about you ...

He deliberately avoided saying he still loved her. He couldn't stand the thought of having her dismiss his feelings.

...Take care, Sim.

His heart was slowing down, so he ordered more espresso and was collecting and paying for it when a message received beep came from his jacket pocket. He guessed as he pulled his phone out that the message would be full of anger and recrimination – that Meredith hadn't taken enough time to think about what he was really trying to say – and, as he read the first line back at his booth, he was right:

You are a fool of the highest order. You are torturing me for a mistake I made years ago and for which I have been sorry every day since. I've reached out and tried to make things right, but you seem to be revelling in all of this; a great opportunity for you to be the deep thinking drama queen you've ALWAYS been. So, stay with Sean for as long as you want – watch shit films and get fat on takeaways, whatever you like. We need to sort out the house and the rest ASAP. M

Simon had, mostly, expected such a reply. He hadn't necessarily expected her to be personally insulting about his character defects, but the throwing back of his ideas and comments was completely predictable. He guessed she probably felt lost and let down and had quite possibly expected him to forgive, forget and move on, but he couldn't ditch the overwhelming sense that he felt like a *fool*, a dupe who has been completely used and treated like a village idiot.

He texted her a reply:

I'm sorry you feel that way about things. Let me know how and when and where you want to sort things out. Sim

He left his espresso, picked up his newspaper and went home on the bus. And on his way home he looked through the Saturday entertainment supplement *The Guide* and made a lightning decision about the next step in his emotional life. No more bus stop liaisons. No more married women in retro-nightclubs. He would use the *Soulmates* section of the newspaper supplement to approach future dates with a more scientific approach – leaving carefully thought out messages about who he was, maybe embellished with some "re-organised" personal details, he would have a chance to stop being a "deep thinking drama queen" for a start, and arrange meetings to suit him.

Chapter 18...

It had been three weeks since Simon had decided to attempt to extricate himself from Meredith. He still didn't feel extricated; he felt bound tightly to his old life and had spent many hours looking through old photographs in the boxes she had sent over. He had begun text after text to her too – deciding to abandon them all at the last moment before he pressed send. Mark had contacted him twice by text:

Saint, Mark here. I do understand your position in all of this. You must be heartbroken. I know I am. And Merry is too. It's a damned awful situation. Is there anything I can do to make things better between the two of you – flagellation? Running through the streets naked? Anything, Saint, name it. I miss seeing you. Mark

Simon replied:

Mark, don't worry. I don't blame you and my guess is that, deep down, neither does Merry. She might still be feeling angry that the truth was exposed, but that isn't your problem – although I appreciate it must feel that way. I miss seeing you too ...

This was only partially true. Simon still felt some resentment for Mark's blabbermouth comments about Dean and wished he could have kept quiet; in that way – even existing inside such a lie – Simon *could* have continued living his life with Meredith.

Two days later Mark texted him again:

Simon, as Merry's dad and your friend I am begging you to try and forgive her – preferably sooner rather than later. She's a mess, Saint, a total sodding mess. Has she spoken to you about the house, your house? I think she's considering renting it out or selling it. Speak soon hopefully. Mark

Simon's jaw tightened as he read the part about selling the house. Meredith *still* hadn't mentioned any thoughts about what to do with their property. He replied to Mark, thinking that perhaps he should be careful from this point on; that maybe Mark was now acting on Meredith's behalf as a go-between:

Mark, don't know anything about the house deal – selling or renting. I guess Meredith isn't thinking straight about that kind of thing, as the house belongs to both of us and she couldn't possibly sell, or even rent it out, without my signature. Who knows, eh? Let me know if you hear anything, ok? Simon

Simon parents were becoming agitated too and he had endured a difficult Sunday lunch with them the day after meeting Judy. He had half-expected them to be on Meredith's side; he had taken the initial blame for leaving, but he was hoping they would consider the best of him and his actions and at the very least give him the benefit of the doubt. But he was wrong.

'So, Simon, when are you and Meredith planning on sorting this thing out?' Simon's father carved the roast beef, sipping his red wine between cuts and glancing back to his son – who sat with a glass of his own, staring in to the liquid and daydreaming. Simon's mother was reading a newspaper but he noticed her look over the top of her glasses, waiting for his answer.

'It's not really a question of *when* we sort things out, dad. It's more of ... *how* we sort this out,' Simon replied, very happy with his answer.

'I don't really understand that,' Simon's mother said. She put her paper down, stood up, refilled her wine glass and sat next to Simon. He felt an immediate sense of annoyance – as if his parents had created a game plan, some kind of tag-team/good cop, bad cop. His father sipped and carved and his mother smiled at him. 'Why a how?' she said.

Simon wanted to say, *'Why a how? That's appalling English, mum.'* But instead he smiled back and said, 'We've reached a difficult point where it's almost impossible to discuss the reasons for being together or not. I know it doesn't make any sense to the two of you, but, with all due respect, it doesn't *need* to make sense to you, only to Merry and me.'

'This is just so frustrating. I've tried to call Meredith, but she won't answer the bloody phone,' Simon's mother said. She swigged a large mouthful of the wine and used the end of her right index finger to wipe away a small amount of the drink left around her top lip.

'Your mother and I are feeling really frustrated, Simon.'

'Yeah, I get that you're frustrated. Sorry about all that frustration, but that's just the way it is. And, to be frank, the more you push me, the more likely I am to tell you even less about anything that happens.'

'But I just don't get why you left her. Why did you? Why Simon, why?' Simon's mother said and tried to hold his hand. He pulled it away.

'Can we talk about something else now, please?' he said.

Chapter 19...

'So you're really going on this lonely-hearts thing tonight, yeah?' Sean said on the morning before Simon's first *Soulmates* arranged date.

'Sure am, pardner. I'm a goin' out to meet me ... Jesus, it's hard, and boring, keeping up the Wild West voice thing,' Simon said, smiling at Sean as they both sat at the kitchen table drinking coffee. A rare morning had found them both able to stay at home and relax, enjoying each other's company before the day began – instead of the usual late night review of a day already spent.

'What do you know about this lovely lady?' Sean asked.

'Well, you are allowed to leave photos online if you like, but we both opted out of that; the element of surprise seems like a reasonable idea ... I think ... I hope. Anyway, she's in theatre production, a stage manager in London and she sounds, on the voicemail thing, really sweet.'

Sean twisted his mouth in curiosity. 'Sweet? Like how?'

'She sounded friendly, bubbly. I don't know, nice, you know?'

'And where is this assignation taking place?'

'London. Restaurant in Soho. Eight-ish. I'll find a toilet excuse later and text you.'

Simon stood up and washed his coffee mug thoroughly. He knew Sean's obsessive compulsiveness might still require a check of his standards of cleanliness, but he did his best. Simon wanted to go into town and buy some new clothes for his big night out. He had a warm feeling inside, that he would meet his date, Cynthia, later and realise at once that *she* was the one and that Meredith's (constant) image in his mind might simply dissolve ...

'Have a good day ... and night,' Sean called out to Simon.

'You too. Any plans for tonight?'

'Meeting a lady myself.'

Simon skipped back into the kitchen. 'Kept that quiet didn't you, addy up, who she be?'

Sean grinned. 'She comes into the store all the time. She's in a band, bass player, kind of cool, looks a bit like Donna Matthews ... you remember, her from Elastica?'

'Yeah, yeah, I remember her, very hot. Sounds promising, looks-wise anyway, very nice. Where are you going?' Simon sat back down.

'Town. Drinks. Movie maybe, maybe not. We shall see.'

'Excellent. Well, if I don't see you later we shall have to use the power of the text *much* later.'

'Fo sho, my man. Ciao,' Sean said.

Simon spent two hours sweating with fashion-anxiety in the town centre, going from shop to shop, and back again to many of them, trying on different shirts and pairs of trousers; being hassled by commission-based sales assistants who wanted to "help" him find the right outfit. Eventually he collapsed into a chair outside Edwards with an espresso in hand, waiting for the caffeine kick in his capillaries.

He closed his eyes and tried to re-summon Cynthia's last voice message, and then convert her words and tone into a face: 'Hi Simon, lovely to get your message. It would be lovely to meet you in London. Soho sounds great, there are so many good places to eat. Shall we meet on Old Compton street, outside *Patisserie Valerie* at eight and just find a place? Or would you like to book somewhere? Either way is lovely by me. Let me know. Really looking forward to meeting you ... bye ... this is Cynthia, bye.'

Simon smiled. She had used the word *lovely* three times. He tried to turn his mind on to her voice, her engaged interest in where they might eat and how excited she sounded about the date. He sipped his drink and looked at the shirt he had just bought – a green, white and blue check-blend, not his usual style, but inoffensive enough to look all right under a jacket and not become a talking point. He had also purchased some expensive hair wax. He had planned to get his hair cut, but time was running out before his planned departure to the big city and he would only just have enough time left to go home, wash and change, and wrestle with his hairstyle – hoping it would be a good-hair day/evening.

He was about to leave when he heard his mobile phone beep a message received alert. He fully expected Sean to text him questions and updates throughout the day and in to the evening. He smiled and took the phone out:

> Hi, it's me. Am feeling very low. Really want to rent out the house and go away for a while. Hope that's ok with you. Text me to let me know. I'll sort out tenants and paperwork. M

Simon sat back and breathed out heavily. Such a clinical text from Meredith – he wouldn't ever get used to those. So cold and business-like. No enquiry about him or his health or feelings. But then he felt a wash of guilt. After all, there he was, sipping coffee outside a cafe, in the sun, with hair wax and a new shirt, about to

go on a date in London. Not exactly cutting a sad figure, was he? He began a reply:

> That's fine with me. If you need me to sign anything or help in any way, let me know. Sorry you're feeling so low. It's all really shitty. A trip away might help. See you. Sim

He sent the text and immediately regretted the sign-off: See you. It struck a note of possible hope to meet in the future, while also held, to him, the emotional clang of gone and lost for ever SEE ... YOU ...

Simon sat and stared at his phone for about ten minutes. He was hoping Meredith would read his text and decide to call him; to tell him she was sorry again and that all she wanted was for him to come home. He would take that; he would take *anything like that* – even a slightly grudging "Come home" plea.

He didn't truly *enjoy* being single; he knew he might one day, but this was *not* that day. Sean had managed to convince him that if he were to accept what Meredith had done with Dean, forgive her unconditionally and not question the manner in which she had handled the post-revelation separation, he would effectively be signing his individuality; his personality and, most importantly, his soul over to a woman who was displaying all the signs of complacency which might include future *transgressions*...future Deans.

The phone didn't ring or beep. He picked it up and went home to wash, change and persuade his hair not to impersonate Liberace's style.

Chapter 20...

Simon saw Cynthia standing by the window of pastries and sweets on display at *Patisserie Valerie*. It was nearly eight o'clock and he had spent the better part of the last ninety minutes convinced he would be late, sprinting between the train and the tube, off the tube, up the escalators, pushing past angry-faced commuters and finally rounding the corner to Old Compton street.

She was about five feet and eight inches tall; short, bobbed red hair and wearing a dark-green military-style *Superdry* jacket over a black skirt and dark-tan boots. He stopped on the corner and tried to focus on her face. He knew he was being superficial but, he reasoned, looks are important to most people. She looked nice – a completely inadequate description for him to describe to someone else, but that was the first word that popped up in his mind: NICE. And nice was good enough, better than good enough. He wiped his forehead dry and looked into the darkened window of the shop next to him. He thought he looked all right, although his fringe had managed to curl into a Tintin meets ski-jump look. He tried to force it to one side but it was sticking to that distinctive shape and he knew he had entered the late-for-a-first-date zone already. He breathed in and out and walked around the corner and across the road towards Cynthia, who was looking at her watch.

'Hi, hello. I'm Simon and I'm very sorry for being a bit late.' He shot out his hand, hoping it wasn't sweaty, and smiled at her.

'That's no problem. Lovely to meet you, Simon. I'm Cynthia.'

They held hands in a slow shake for a few seconds; Simon trying not to crush her slender fingers. His father had always gone on at him about the value of a strong handshake.

'Shall we find somewhere to eat, I'm famished,' Cynthia said. Simon nodded a yes and followed her lead – across the road to

a place called *Amalfi*. They were shown to a window table and offered menus as they sat down.

'Wine?' the waiter asked.

'May we see the list, please?' Cynthia said. The waiter smiled and nodded and brought back a long, laminated sheet.

Simon wondered if he should perhaps stick to orange juice or something equally as soft after the Sarah Marshall debacle. He worried that alcohol was a guarantee of blabbermouthy disaster. But as he glanced at the studious way Cynthia was taking the lead on ordering just the right vintage, he thought it would be rude to deny such a mutual pleasure as sharing a nice drink with a new friend/acquaintance.

'I was thinking about ordering a Chilean Merlot, any thoughts on that? Any preferences?' Cynthia said, smiling and looking him directly in the eye.

'Nope. I'm a bit of a wine philistine, I'm afraid. Red or white is the extent of my vino epicurean standards,' Simon said the words and wondered what they meant – why did his mouth always insist on running away like that? Cynthia laughed, obviously thinking he *was* funny and in a way that made him assume she thought he was a sweet, funny man. Thank god for a positive interpretation, he thought, smiling back at her.

'Merlot, please,' Cynthia said to the waiter who had returned without Simon noticing.

The wine arrived as quickly as the menus and wine list and they were soon sipping away and, Simon assumed, evaluating each other.

'So, how many times have you arranged a *Soulmates* date?' Cynthia asked him. She leaned forwards, put her elbows on the table and smiled so that her eyes lit up with curiosity.

Simon wasn't sure if there was an etiquette to moments and questions like this one. Should he answer that this was his first time. Or was he supposed to behave like a battle-scarred General; fresh out of one tour of duty in blind-date hell and about to go back to the frontline as a veteran of the love campaign? He took an uneducated guess and leapt in with both feet.

'First time for me. Very nerve-wracking too. How about you?' he said; thinking he had replied too quickly.

'Third time for me. I work odd hours and I don't get much chance to socialise outside of the theatre.'

'I would have assumed there were loads of lovely people to meet in the theatrical world. Lots of artistic, interesting types?' Simon deliberately mirrored back the word *lovely*. He hoped she had missed it. And anyway who appropriated a word like *lovely*?

'There are lots of *loveys*, not always that lovely, though. I've been out with a few actors, but they're usually egomaniacs who want to be the centre of everything you do together.'

'That sounds pretty grim. How did the first couple of *Soulmates* dates go?'

Cynthia looked a bit uncomfortable with the question and Simon knew he had gone against that etiquette he didn't know existed. Was this how you learned about it – go on a few dates, mess things up with some really nice women and eventually plateau with some knowledge in hand about the do's and don'ts of the *Soulmates* world?

Cynthia poured herself some more wine and offered some to Simon; he nodded and waited – half-expecting her to throw it in his face and walk out. Was this to be another Sarah Marshall moment?

'They went okay, but obviously not as well as they could have or I wouldn't be here,' she said. She smiled at him warmly and he felt the strain of social humiliation drain away.

'These things are so hard, aren't they? I mean, thrown together in a pressure-filled situation like a blind date and then, like me

right now, creating even more tension by becoming all post-modern and shining a bright light on that stress,' Simon said. Cynthia almost spurted wine across the table; she laughed until tears formed and touched Simon's hand. He laughed too, telling himself he had *meant* to be the funny guy; the clown who took all the horror out of the faux-pas-riddled world of the dating game. He wasn't sure he had been *that* funny, but he was thrilled Cynthia thought so.

'Jesus, that was fantastic, Simon. Do you write at all?' Cynthia said. She wiped her eyes dry and suddenly seemed full of energy – looking straight at him; completely engaged in waiting for his reply. He realised he felt flattered and hadn't felt so *listened* to for a long time. And then he thought of how Sean might answer such a question; that his best friend would, doubtless, use this opening as a launchpad to move things along – and potentially to the bedroom – finding angles and untruths to ease the way.

'I do, yes, I write sketches, skits. I haven't done much lately, been very busy running my bookshop.'

'Yes, of course, the bookshop. I love bookshops! I'd love to read some of your work. Would you send it to me?'

Simon smiled and imagined himself trying to find obscure pieces of dramatic humour to claim as his own. Plagiarism = sex-life?

'Sure. But let's talk about you for a bit. You work as a stage manager, do you want to direct? And what other interests do you have?'

Cynthia seemed happy to accept the spotlight. She sat back.

'I love the theatre. I studied theatrical management at the Guildhall school and I've been in love with the entire concept of public dramatisation since I was a girl. Directing? Well, maybe, but I get such a buzz from what I do; drawing all the plans up for the make-up of the production, from the ground up sort of thing.

And then the opening night and the applause. It's like a drug. Do you know that feeling, the sense of completeness, elation?'

'Sure. The finished product, amazing,' Simon replied. 'I grew up with people around me telling me I should become an actor, mainly because of my name, but still ...'

'What, because you're called Simon?'

'No, no,' he laughed. 'My full name's Simon Templar.' Simon waited for the television series moment of realisation in Cynthia's face – it didn't come.

'Sorry, I'm not sure what that means,' she said.

'Oh right. There was a popular telly series called *The Saint*, it was developed from a bunch of books, and the lead character was called Simon Templar. He was a sort of James Bond-type, but he didn't work for the British government, or any other government.'

Simon let the explanation tail off at that point. He could see Cynthia had no recollection of the show or the books, and didn't seem at all interested. He wondered whether he should try and let rip with another post-modern joke.

'So, do you have any other things you love outside of the theatre,' he asked quickly.

'Absolutely I do. My other love is the straight-edge life.'

'What's that all about?'

Cynthia furrowed her eyebrows in disbelief that Simon would need to ask such a question. He wondered if she was drunk.

'Straight-edge is about total freedom of expression. A love of God and life and all the natural highs, without the need for drugs or booze. It's about music and friendship and belief, you know, real faith.'

'But you're drinking wine?'

'I'm not perfect, true. I love wine, but I don't drink it very often and I don't let it abuse my body. Do you think you might want to find out more about straight-edging?'

'Yeah, sounds interesting. Definitely a maybe. How did you get into it?' Simon's mind was swirling now. He could feel a sweat building under his arms and a memory from childhood: his mother telling him never to answer the front door without her – in case The Moonies took him away to their cult camps. Was Cynthia using *Soulmates* to recruit new disciples to this straight-edge thing? What had happened to those two previous dates? Were they locked in a darkened room; shivering, naked and bruised, being slowly *converted*?

'From my old boyfriend. He was crazy for the lifestyle. It took me a long time to see the real value of it after he died, but now it *is* my life. It's the most amazing experience ever and there are some of the most lovely, creative people you could hope to meet.'

Simon almost laughed aloud in shock and distress: Ah, ha ha. The boyfriend had *died*! Or had he been sacrificed by the other straight-edgers in a Wicker Man style scenario? He imagined his exit strategy: a seal-like bark emitting from his vocal cords and then perhaps a dive from the restaurant window next to them. A forward-roll and on to his feet, pounding the pavement back to the railway station – back home. Sean. Safety.

'Sounds good, fantastic. I'm just going to use the loo. Be back in a moment.'

Cynthia winked at him.

Simon found the toilets; locked himself in a cubicle and began a text to Sean:

> HELP! She's a nutter. She's a religious zealot recruiter, trying to get me to join a cult, drug-free thing. Aaarrghhh! Am locked in a cubicle. Should I climb out of the window or make my polite excuses and leave? I need to find a happy place. Can feel a foetal moment coming on!

Sean replied quickly:

Fuck-a-doodley. Get out. Get out now. Say you don't feel well, something you ate – before they eat you! – that you'll call her, pay the bill and leave. LEAVE!

Simon walked back to the table smiling – a fake grin; attempting to mix in some show of inner pain. Cynthia saluted him and held her wine glass aloft. He nodded.

'Cynthia, I'm so sorry about this, I have to go. I was sick in the toilet and I feel really lousy now. Maybe I could walk you to your tube stop and we could do this again another time?'

Cynthia looked at him blankly, as if she were expecting him to make a drum roll/cymbal smash noise at the end of such a joke.

'Is that okay with you, if we pay the bill and leave?' Simon said. He was feeling more and more paranoia building – and began to wonder if there might be a van of straight-edger heavies waiting outside to pull him in and begin his conversion.

'Well I suppose that's a *bit* different to the mobile phone ringing or beeping an *urgent* message. But it's still a lame excuse,' Cynthia said. She motioned to the waiter and he brought the bill over. 'Just go, I'll pay and put it down to more bullshit experience,' she said.

'What does *that* mean?' Simon said, his voice sounding higher than he ever wanted to hear it. Even though he had been caught lying, he still felt a burn of indignity that he should be *called* a liar by this complete stranger.

'Oh, what could it *mean*, Simon? What does it all *mean*? What do you think? You guys make me sick, and I mean really sick, not like your phoney sick in the loo thing. You think you can make your ignorant judgments based on looks and clothes and the size of a girl's breasts, that nothing she says or does matters. It's all about the superficial, yeah? So what was it that ruined the evening? My

teeth? My hairstyle? What?' Cynthia was beginning to shout.

Simon glanced over his shoulder at the restaurant door. How many more evenings would he have to endure like this one, like the one with Sarah Marshall? Was he *so* deluded that, although he could see the way he had been too *honest* with Sarah Marshall had ruined that date, and his cult/obsession fears were to blame on this occasion, he really didn't feel as if he had *really* lied and cheated and invested that much in either women. He hadn't promised anything, and he had, at the very least, been respectful enough not to waste their time any further than the one evening – or at least *one* part of *one* evening; he hadn't gotten as far as dessert yet.

'It's nothing like that. I *am* feeling ill. I was sick and I really don't like being spoken to like a wanker when I'm not being one. I have a rare condition called Addison's Disease, and vomiting is one of the early onset signs of an episode. I need to go now, I'm afraid. Thanks for agreeing to meet me,' Simon said the words slowly and carefully and looked Cynthia in the eye as he spoke.

He had learned about Addison's Disease from his uncle who had recently been diagnosed. He checked the total on the bill and laid down more than his fifty percent. Guilt didn't have an exact price, but it would *have* to be more than half.

Cynthia looked surprised by his calm 'honesty'. She finished her wine and bit her bottom lip. 'I'm sorry, Simon. I'm truly sorry. I've had some crappy dates recently and I'm feeling very vulnerable. I almost didn't come this evening because of the date-crapness ratio. Do you need me to call you a taxi, or an ambulance?'

'No, no, that's okay, but thanks.' Simon felt like the worst kind of low lying dirty dog. He wondered how far down he would go to extract himself from a hellish situation – whether he too would sink to the level of cheating a loving partner the way Meredith had done. Human frailty wasn't ever going to be predictable and he hated that.

Simon texted Sean as he caught two tubes back to Paddington Station:

Total disaster. She went apeshit at me when I said I wanted to leave – called me a typical male knobhead (which I was being, let's be honest about that) and when I embellished my lie – telling her I have Addison's, that disease my uncle has – she was sooo nice to me; helped me find a taxi, wished me the best, kiss on the cheek and asked me to text her when I got home. Painful stuff, feel like a total scummer now. Am a total scummer. Actually feel as if what Merry did wasn't so bad. Hope things better where you are.

Sean replied:

Don't sweat the small stuff, bro-ho. Merry lied and screwed another guy for SIX MONTHS! No comparison, none! You didn't feel like it tonight and you were honest about not wasting her time. You paid your way and that's the roll of the dice, mi amigo (no, I'm not sure what the hell that means either, but it sounds good, eh?) Things good here, see you tomorrow evening.

As his first train arrived, he realised how completely *stupid* he had been, how much he had overreacted regarding the straight-edge idea – were their objectives so whacky, a belief in the goodness of others and respecting yourself? Cynthia had been so nice to him, and did it matter that she was passionate about her convictions? Surely passion and dedication were *good* things?

As he unlocked Sean's front door, the only thing he could feel content about was the fact that he hadn't felt any true attraction for Cynthia. He guessed she would find someone much better suited to that life than he would ever be and more than ready to dive in to a full-blown relationship with her and her straight-edge.

He had begun to realise that he just wanted to have some FUN.

Chapter 21...

When Simon got home from work the following day Sean was already waiting for him; two beers opened.

'Jeez, you're early. I don't think I've ever known you leave work before six,' Simon said. He tossed his rucksack to one side and slumped on to the uncomfortable sofa. 'How did things go last night? I guessed you made out pretty well, staying away and ...'

Simon stopped talking and looked at Sean; he looked pale and upset.

'You okay?' Simon asked.

Sean threw back a swig of the beer and passed the other bottle to Simon.

'Got something to tell you. Something bad,' Sean said.

'Oh god, is someone pregnant? Do you need me to leave?'

'Not like that, not about me. Judy came to see me today. She was upset and needed to talk ...'

'You and Judy? Are you two?'

'No, man, nothing like that. Listen for a second, okay. She was upset and wanted me to tell you something about Merry.'

'Is she all right? Is she hurt?' Simon sat up and put the beer bottle on the floor.

'No, if only. She's ... she's seeing some other guy.' Sean breathed out long and hard; seeming as if he had completed the hardest task of his life and pushed himself to the most excruciating limits of endurance.

Simon sat and stared at his best friend for a few seconds. He was aware of his heartbeat: a-boom, booooom, bang, bam!

'Is it Dean, this other guy?' he said; his voice husky.

'Don't know any details. Judy wouldn't tell me jackshit. I'm so sorry. This is shit, so shit. Are you okay? Silly question, yeah?'

'Fuckly buggering,' Simon said. 'I mean, I know I'm off trying to sow some oats, and failing big time, *every* time. But she was supposed to be mourning me and finding herself and being there for us to ...' his voice trailed off and then picked up again just as Sean leaned in to say something. 'All the stupidity of young people, like us, who don't try hard enough, and ... oh fuckity fuck it. Well, that's fine, well done, Merry, last laugh to you. That's just dandy dan.'

'Sim, man. I know it seems shite now, but things will ...'

'I know, like the D-ream song says: "Things will only get better ..." Blah, blah. Well let's see, eh? More beer, pizza and *Fight Club*? Okay with you?' Simon said.

'Do you want to talk about this some more?' Sean asked.

'Nope, thanks, but no. I'm okay for now.'

Sean nodded, smiled and went off to collect the pizza menu and two more beers. Simon stood, took his jacket off and pulled the DVD box from the shelf. He forced himself to seem happy and light on his feet, but the film suggestion was where his mind was placed at that precise moment. He *wanted* to feel the pummel of a fist connecting with the bridge of his nose; the slam of knuckles in his belly and the collapse of his legs as he keeled over – because he knew physical pain was the only way to divert the pain in his head and heart about Meredith.

Simon only half-watched; half-enjoyed the film.

Sean sloped off to call his new guitarist girlfriend as the credits rolled and Simon decided to check his *Soulmates* voice messages; anything to take his thoughts on to something new: 'Hi, my name's Catrina, with a C. I live in London. I'm a costume designer for film and television and I usually don't have a lot of time to socialise. I really liked your message, I think James Cameron's earlier films were so much better than the recent ones too. I was wondering if you might like to meet somewhere and talk, chat, eat ... well,

anyway, if you want to, call me. My number is ...'

Simon liked the sound of her voice – soft, mellifluous (his favourite word in the dictionary). He looked at his hand.

'Should I call her now?'

'Who, Merry?' the hand said.

'Not sodding Merry, no. Call Catrina, with a C?'

'Ah, *that* her. Sure, why not?'

Simon dialled the number from the voice message and waited. His heart was pounding again – ring, ring, then a click. He was just about to begin a prepared opening when he realised he had reached an ansaphone: 'Hi, Catrina and Jenny are out at the moment. Please leave a message ...'

A message, no human contact! This was better than a voice-to-voice first meeting. He had assumed, waiting for the call to be answered, that his charm had flatlined at that point: 'Hi, hello, this is a message for Catrina ... with a C, unlike Hurricane ... anyway, sorry about that. My name's Simon Templar, you left me a message. I'd love to meet and chat. If you want to give me a call back, my number is ...'

Simon put his mobile back in his jacket and sat forward. He placed his face in his hands and silently screamed; he didn't want to disturb Sean – who was chatting and laughing happily upstairs. He screamed without sound at the emotional hell he found himself drifting in over Meredith's *new start;* mostly through sadness and despair, but partly from jealousy. How long would her new boyfriend last? How had she found someone else so damn fast? Was it Dean – had the *tonguey* creepo been waiting around all this time?

And he screamed at his own verbal ineptitude – why couldn't he stop himself mentioning Hurricane Katrina on the message? Because, after all, he *never* tired of people abusing/amusing *his* name!

Simon was about to leave the room; his hand hovered over the light switch. He didn't want to make a production of going to bed when Sean was getting more and more verbally intimate with his new girl. But Simon had reached his limit of wince-inducing moments on that day, and besides, he wanted to get in to the bathroom before Sean, who had a habit of falling asleep in the bath and lying behind the locked door – in the room with the only toilet in the house – for hours. Simon clicked the light switch off and then the phone rang.

For a moment he imagined it would be Meredith crowing about her new boyfriend: *'Oh he's so much bigger and better than you ever were. And he has such a wide tongue, like a Blue whale!'*

'Hi,' he said quietly.

'Hello? ... hi, this is Catrina, you just left me a message. At least I think it was you. Is this Simon Templar?'

'Yes it's me, Simon, hi. Good to speak to you at last. I hate leaving message after message.'

'Me too. Really nice to hear your message, though.'

'I just want to say how sorry I am about my lamentable attempt at so-called humour, when I linked your name to Hurricane Katrina, with a K of course. It was nerves and basic male stupidity, I'm afraid, such a disaster of a comment,' Simon thought he sounded charmingly apologetic and Catrina laughed which made him finally able to sit down and begin the process of relaxing.

'That's okay. I got it a lot after the storm, and *you* must have had plenty of stick over the years about your name, too. Which of the two actors are you more like, Roger Moore or Ian Ogilvy?'

'Far from both. And yep, certainly have had my naming and shaming moments, got my dad to thank for that. That was another reason for me feeling so guilty after the message.'

'So ... would you like to meet up soon?'

Simon took a moment and thought of Sarah Marshall and

Cynthia and wondered if he should only agree after a solid process of interviewing Catrina: Any problems with a still-broken-hearted guy trying to overcome the pain of an ex-partner shagging some new bloke by bouncing around the *Soulmates* column and seeking out a new love; renewed passion and some new body to hold through the night to numb the agony of suddenly-singledomness? No? Great! Any religious/cult affiliations that may lead to me being chained to a dungeon drainpipe and brainwashed in to providing my first-born for sacrifice? No? Maybe? Yes! Raincheck ...

'That sounds great. Shall we meet this week?'

'Cool, the weekend perhaps, Saturday afternoon?'

'Lovely, where would suit you?'

'There's a nice marquee with food and drink outside the National Film Theatre, it's a big celebration of British film or something. We could have lunch there?'

'Sounds nice. Shall we say one o'clock?' Simon said and smiled. He was enjoying the ease of the arrangement and he liked Catrina's voice.

'Fab. Shall we exchange mobile numbers so that we can confirm things and let each other know we've arrived, that sort of thing?'

Simon wondered briefly if the number exchange might also prove to be a ruse – a way to call his number at one-ish, spot him and make a quick decision to stay or go; or was that just something *he* might do? He realised in an instant that it *was* something he could employ.

Numbers were exchanged.

'So, see you on Saturday. And I promise, no idiotic name jokes,' Simon said.

Catrina laughed again. Simon heard another female voice in her background and wondered if she was fortunate enough to have her own version of Sean.

'See you then, Saint Simon,' she said.

Simon thought about his *lack* of Sainthood prospects; then of Mark, almost certainly still bereft at the separation and his part in it. And then, as he made for the bathroom – giving a thumbs-up to Sean as he walked past his bedroom – he thought about Meredith, and to their house. Their rented-out house.

He felt a rush of anger. He would text Judy now – she had become a natural arbiter – and ask her to give Meredith a message: he wanted the house sold; the final bond between them broken:

Hi Judy, got the joyous news about Merry (widow) – bad joke, I know, and the new guy. Pretty swift work there, eh? Good for her! Love is all around, apparently. I'm ecstatic about that particular piece of news because it's pushed a button that needed pushing (yes, I know I'm rambling!) I would like to ask you to pass on a message to Merry for me (I'm not feeling polite at the moment). I want the house sold NOW. I want out of the whole thing. I'm more than happy to start the process with estate agents and the rest. I just need her to agree ... Sim xx

A reply beeped in soon after:

Jesus, Simon. I know you're upset and I completely understand why, but selling the house is a BIG thing. Is that really what you want? J xx

Simon typed his message back hastily and then switched his phone off:

Yes. Yes. Yes. Please pass the message on. Hope you're ok, Judy. I miss seeing you. S xx

Chapter 22...

Simon woke the next morning to find two texts received – one from Judy, which read:

> Okay, I'll tell her, although I would rather NOT be in the middle all the time – the messenger DOES end up getting killed. And I miss you too. I miss you and Merry together. This is the worst case scenario made flesh. Am beginning to cry again. Hopefully c u soon. Best to that reprobate friend of yours! J xxxx

And the other text was from Meredith. Simon didn't open it immediately; he lingered for a few minutes, making a big deal of a small task – grinding coffee beans. Sean had left already. A post-it note on the front door read: May not be back tonight, another "guitar lesson"!

Simon toasted a bagel and then got dressed and brushed his teeth. He eventually decided to have a look at Meredith's message on the train as he travelled to work:

> Judy told me what you want. I think that kind of Breaking News should really be dealt with by us, between us – don't you agree? Judy is really stressed about this whole mess. Fine about the house. Beyond caring right now. Would you mind if I deal with the tenants and the estate agents? – I've built up a good rapport with them. Again, I don't really mind either way. M

Simon bit down on his right index finger to stop himself shouting out one of the many expletives pounding through his skull. Why was Meredith so intent on punishing *his* every move? Did she truly have so little remaining compassion or contrition for any of this? As far as he knew, she didn't know about his recent *Soulmates* dates – and hopefully she would *never* find out about

Sarah Marshall; he would never play badminton at that club again either. So why did she continue to think *he* should be treated like such a schmuck?

He decided to fire back a text without thinking the whole thing through – no over-analysing the nuances of each phrase and the emotional impact on the reader. He would just write what he was feeling and send it away – like the Russian Roulette texts he and Sean used to send. It would feel good, liberating. He might even make her think twice about where to apportion future blame. He wrote his thoughts down quickly and sent the text as soon as the final letter was tapped – no spelling, grammar or punctuation checks, just fire at will!

Message sent, he read on the screen. And then he read his text:

> Fuck whether you're beyond caring. Fuck the rapport you have with tenants living in our home. And fuck your new boyfriend – which I'm sure you do on a regular basis. Fine, you deal with the house sale. Let's just lay it all in a grave and bury it. Let me know when it's done. S

There was no reply from Meredith.

Later that day, as Simon tried to find some comfort on the awful sofa – re-watching Orson Welles, larger-than-life, in *Touch of Evil* – he received a text from Judy:

> WTF?! Why oh why oh why did you send that shitty text to Merry? Simon, come on, just keep that crap to yourself for now and concentrate on re-building something good in your life. J x

Only one kiss – Judy's classic *kiss-off.*

Chapter 23...

Saturday arrived and Simon had been up and awake, bought *The Guardian* and begun to peruse the latest *Soulmates* ads with a cup of coffee. He was determined to take life very easy on that day, before he suddenly realised – as if a bucket of ice-cold water had been poured over his head and then the bucket had been crumpled on to his scalp – that he had very little time to get to London and meet Catrina with a C.

He rushed around the house, cleaning his mug and plate and checking the work surfaces for spills and stains. Sean's obsessive-compulsiveness always got worse when he was heavily involved with a new woman – his need for order became amplified the harder he fell for the woman-in-question.

Then Simon began making up his mind on which jacket to wear, only to change it again as he started to re-style his hair, which seemed to have decided to rise on one side and cling to his head on the other. He had no time to fiddle-faddle about, although, as he walked to the railway station he muttered to himself about his extreme ability to faff about for England when most pressed for time.

The journey went reasonably smoothly, but the tube stations were packed and hot, and Simon found himself daydreaming about the amount of bacteria on the tube-train carriage armrests and the yellow pole-grips.

He eventually made his way across Waterloo Bridge towards the Southbank, and he wondered what kind of red-faced, crazy-haired sight Catrina might be confronted with if he entered the marquee immediately.

He had fifteen minutes to spare and used all of them in the toilets of the National Film Theatre; walking towards the huge photograph of Boris Karloff as Frankenstein's monster next to the *Gents* entrance door. He splashed cool water on his face and breathed out, looking into the over-lit, wall-length mirror in front of him. There wasn't anyone else around, so he used some water to push and press at his head. He closed his eyes in the hope of finding calm. Breathe, breathe.

And then he walked in to the foyer again and pulled out his mobile phone. *One missed call.* Why hadn't he heard it coming in? Damnation, the phone was on silent! Catrina had called him a few minutes before – he called her back.

'Hey there,' she said.

'Hi, are you waiting for me?'

'Yeah, I know it's only a couple of minutes past one, but I was a bit worried you might have changed your mind or got lost.'

'No, no. I should be with you in a minute. Are you in the marquee?'

'Yeah, I'm by the entrance, wearing a black dress. I've got black hair. See you in a minute. Bye.'

'Bye.'

Simon had the, slightest, upper hand. He knew where she was and what she looked like. He could, if he chose to be a devious git, have a peek and make his mind up about staying. But he didn't want to do that. He wanted to have a good time, finally leave his anxieties in the toilet and just seize the day. Wasn't that what everyone else was doing? Simon took one last look in to a reflective photograph – of Errol Flynn – and prodded at his hair; then walked with fake confidence towards the marquee. He spotted Catrina instantly; she was very beautiful; carefully made-up – her eyes reminded him of Elizabeth Taylor's. And she was sitting with a serene smile, which he guessed must be for show – who could be *serene* in a situation such as this?

'Hi, you must be Catrina,' Simon said, holding out his hand. He

was suddenly aware his palm was still a bit damp.

'Catrina took it, 'Nice to meet you, Simon.'

'Would you like a drink?'

'Yes, please, a gin and tonic,' she said. 'Shall we order some food, too?'

'Maybe a drink then food?' Simon wasn't hungry, but had a cold reminder down his spine of his inability to hold his liquor on an empty stomach. He would opt for an orange juice.

'Sure.'

Simon walked off to the bar and placed his order. He looked back at the table, smiled and then realised Catrina was writing a text. Was she contacting her flatmate and begging for a false-emergency to extract her from dealing with him for too long? He pulled out his own mobile and texted Sean:

> Here and ordering drinks. She is lovely, very beautiful, think Liz Taylor in Cat on a Hot Tin Roof. Just one smallish prob (apart from me not being Paul Newman). We've only just met, I'm awaiting the drinks and I've just noticed her writing a text as soon as I walked away – is that a sure sign of: I'm with ugly-bug-boy, get me out of here!?

Sean replied quickly – Simon loved that his best friend knew instinctively that Simon was under time pressure after his comment about being at the bar waiting:

> No. No. And no. It might mean lots of other things too. It might mean: He looks fantastic. Do we need milk? Or even, his flies are open – wow! Don't presume anything. Although, to be fair and honest, it might also mean: I'm with ugly-bug-boy, get me out of here! But that ain't you. You are a dude. Stay the course ... bon chance, amigo. Let me know later.

Simon smiled and replied:

Do we need milk? My flies are sealed, just checked. Ciao.

Sean's message was swift:

Ha, ha! Keep your legs down and your trousers up.

Simon returned to the table and put the drinks down. He smiled at Catrina and tried to read her return smile.

'So you're a costume designer; that sounds brilliant. Have you worked for any big names?' Simon said, and then realised that although he had meant to sound engaged, interested and genuine, he might have made the question sound loaded: that if Catrina *hadn't* worked for any big names she might think he was calling her a failure – not the best opening line. Fortunately for his heart rate she seemed completely relaxed and behaved as if she was used to answering this same question.

'Yep. I've done costumes for theatre, television series and loads of feature films. I did the design for the new Kylie video.'

'Good stuff. Do you get to go to the sets and mix it up with the stars?' And now Simon was *certain* he was asking stupid questions – a blend of sycophancy and the babble of the star-struck. Be cool, he thought, be ice cold. Act aloof about the drama stuff. What's next, are you going to ask her to get you a part in a film?

'Not really. I do a series of fittings and have conversations about the designs and styling with the actors, singers, whoever it is, but it's all very professional. These people get shouted at and photographed all day long and they certainly wouldn't want some cringing and fawning designer-type. You work in a bookshop, is that right?'

'I manage it, yes, that's right.'

'It must be lovely working with books, great ideas, beautiful objects. What's your favourite book?' Catrina asked him. She sipped

her gin and tonic and looked into his eyes. *Her* eyes seemed to brighten with the energy of new endeavour and he began to think everything must be all right now – that her text might have been telling a friend how nice he looked, maybe even intelligent. This was the good-side to his new dating life; the positive outcomes, the sugar and spice layers of getting-to-know-you. He thought he would *swoon*; as if he was caught in an opposing gender-role in some salacious Eighteenth-century novella. He really didn't like the word "swoon" at all and tried to think of a synonym. Just answer the question, Simon! his mind shouted him back in to reality.

'*Revolutionary Road*, by ...'

'Richard Yates, yeah, I read that. It's such a tragically beautiful book. Great film too. I loved his other one, *Easter Parade*, too. He really knew how to write for women. I guess that must be a hugely difficult thing for a male writer.'

She loved Richard Yates!

Simon suddenly remembered Sarah Marshall asking him the same question about books – three dates ago. Had he really been on three dates, including this one, since he and Meredith had separated?

'Yeah, it is. I mean, it must be. I know Nick Hornby's got a thing for Yates too. And, of course, he tried the male writer creating leading female narrator in *How to be Good*. But I really didn't think it was *that* good.'

Catrina laughed and Simon realised he had unintentionally made a pun on the Hornby title. He made a face of: "Hey, I'm a funny guy, that's me, Coco the Clown!"

'You know, I was looking at the menu here earlier and I don't think it's that great, not much variety and all very expensive. Shall we walk across the bridge and get some Italian or something,' Catrina asked.

Simon was about ready to howl like a cartoon dog and bark out the words: Yeah, yeah, yeah! 'Italian sounds great. Any preferences where?' he said.

'Somewhere near, I'm starving,' Catrina said and smiled. She touched his hand, finished her drink and stood up. Simon followed her lead. He gestured a *Ladies first* hand signal for Catrina and they walked towards Waterloo bridge.

They ate pizzas and garlic bread, drank Chianti – Simon couldn't resist doing his Anthony Hopkins as Hannibal Lector fava beans quote – and slowly they began to finish each other's sentences, like old friends meeting again after many years.

At one point, on his way back from the toilet – thankfully not that drunk, just cheerfully *uplifted* by the wine – he looked at his mobile phone, which he had put on silent, and was surprised to see they had been in the restaurant for two and a half hours. He felt as if they had only just begun to touch on the traditional opener topics: job, family, living in London, relationships. Simon had made certain, when the chat was flowing freely, that he did not mention any previous *Soulmates* dates he had been on or ask Catrina about her track record.

'So, Simon Templar, what do you fancy doing now?' Catrina said, still laughing. He had just finished his favourite anecdote, about accidentally making Kate Winslet's nose bleed in a *Pizza Express* in Reading in 1996, when she was on a break from filming *Titanic*. They had had mutual friends – a meal for twenty people across five tables, Simon had been seated next to Winslet and had felt too shy to talk to her. He had noticed the actress had dropped her napkin; leaned down to pick it up at the exact moment Kate had decided to do the same and managed to headbutt her. His mortification was made complete as he tried to apply the napkin to her trickling nose and she had screamed in his face. 'And she called you a shitty shithead?' Catrina asked, bursting in to

laughter again as Simon nodded and pulled a "What are you gonna do?" face. 'And, of course, the weird symmetry that she and Leo joined forces again after *Titanic* and played the Wheelers in *Revolutionary Road*. Odd stuff.'

'Maybe a movie or a gallery?' he said, uncertain he wanted to do either – he was full of food and drink and was enjoying the sitting and talking.

'We could go back to my flat, it's in Camden. My flatmate's away for a few days. We could have coffee or a walk, or just ... you know, chat and stuff?'

Simon *thought* she was making a pass at him – it *seemed* so obvious. He didn't know for certain because he had been very wrong about moments like this before: the character-crushing leaning in for a kiss; only to see the face you are leaning towards curling in to barely concealed disgust.

'That sounds really nice. Let's go shall we?'

Chapter 24...

Simon insisted on paying and they left. He hailed a taxi and they set off for Camden.

'I hope you don't mind, I just have to answer an email,' Catrina said, holding up her iPhone. Simon smiled and nodded. He took out his mobile. Sean had left him a message:

So? How are things? Went the day well?

Simon replied:

Things VERY good, on the way back to her EMPTY flat. Feeling nervous as hell. She is VERY beautiful and funny and cool and sexy and sophisticated and ... sitting next to me! Hope I don't make an idiot of myself. AGAIN.

Catrina gave the taxi driver final instructions about where to pull in. She pointed to a front door and Simon took his wallet out, tipping the driver an extra few pounds. He quickly swung from the cab feeling like the richest guy in town to the horrible realisation that he would almost certainly be broke until his next pay-day.

The interior of the flat was styled in Art Deco – Simon had leafed through a book on the subject at work once and was able to make some reasonably well-informed noises about how good the place looked. Catrina filled a cafetiere and brought through a tray of coffee and cups for them.

As Simon tried to keep the chatter interesting and funny he began to feel a weight of expectation in the air. Nothing had been discussed, no kisses had been exchanged or even a hand held, but the look on Catrina's face made him feel a surge of sexual energy and nearly enough confidence to feel as if he should make a move on her – that she wanted him too. Catrina was seated on the sofa opposite him.

He took a last sip of his coffee, put his cup on the table next to his sofa and stood up. He walked over to Catrina and sat down next to her. Without truly thinking about anything, he leaned in to her neck and began to kiss her. He half-expected her to pull away, stand up and shout, "Uurrgh" then throw him out of the window. But she seemed to be enjoying what he was doing and within minutes she was leading him in to her bedroom.

The first time they had sex Simon felt self-conscious and selfish – lust got the better of him and it was all over fairly quickly. They lay on top of her bed and chatted about how stressful the dating-game was and how it was amazing to meet someone in the afternoon and end up in bed with them later that day. They reassured each

other that this wasn't how they both usually went about meeting people and that the connection they had discovered on this day truly meant something. And then, when he was as certain as he could be that his body wouldn't let him down, Simon began to "meet" Catrina all over again.

Chapter 25...

The next morning, after washing the dishes they had used for a Chinese takeaway, Simon made some toast and coffee for Catrina and took it to her in bed.

'Good morning,' he said, placing the cup on her bedside table. She stretched and smiled at him.

'Morning. How did you sleep?' she said, sipping the coffee and nibbling the toast. He sat down on the bed and smoothed the duvet next to her shoulder.

'Good, very well. You?'

She nodded and took a larger mouthful of the toast.

'Would you like to do something today, maybe have lunch, catch a movie?' Simon asked. He had brought a cup of coffee for himself too and drank it eagerly, feeling full of energy; feeling lucky to be in the presence of such a beautiful woman who was naked and smiling at him.

'I'm really sorry, Simon, I can't do much of anything today except work. I've got a job that needs finishing by tomorrow morning. I may have to work through the night. It's the peril of being self-employed.'

Simon shrugged and smiled at her.

'That's cool, totally fine. I'll head off after breakfast. Perhaps we could meet again sometime next week?'

Catrina nodded and smiled but didn't say anything – which left Simon with a sinking feeling.

He leaned in to her and kissed her mouth. They had quick sex and then Simon left – Catrina had showered and changed and begun to work in the time it took him to put his clothes back on and take the cups and plate back to the kitchen where he washed them.

Travelling back home Simon fought all the negative impulses in his brain – there wasn't any reason to suspect he was being played by Catrina; after all what exactly had she promised him? They were new friends/sex partners/ friends with benefits. All he had to do was be cool; wait for her to text him – she had said she would – and then they could hook-up again. This was going to be a *good* thing. He could make up his character as he went along; no embellishments or lies. And hopefully no Deans in the background!

He had taken a photograph of Catrina on his mobile phone – he looked at it and knew his father would think he had "Done well" meeting such a lovely looking woman. Simon texted Sean and attached the photograph of Catrina:

> Goooood morning, Vietnam! How's it hangin'? On my way home after a very nice night of great sex with a beautiful woman. The sun is shining through the train window, I've bought The Observer to read later and I feel happiness in my cynical veins. How are you? Did you spend a night of lust with the geetar-girl?

Sean replied:

> Very nice, amigo. You are indeed a happy one. Seriously though, that's great news. Thanks for the photo too – she is VERY beautiful. Jeez, you got lucky there. And yes, I did spend the

night with Emily (that's her name – feel bad referring to her as the guitar girl). I know this might sound insane, but I genuinely think I'm falling for her. Later, dude.

Simon wrote his reply with raised eyebrows of surprise:

Man alive, that's amazing news – and you are sooo matter-of-fact about it. You might be in LOVE with Emily. Good for you. Brilliant news. Would love to see a photo of her and meet her asap. Later back to you, duderooni.

Simon read his newspaper and tried to concentrate his mind on the articles, but all he could think about was Catrina, her life in London, how he might have found a future with her. He began to think of ideas, ways of impressing her, making her see him as the "one" she had to be with. His train pulled in to the station.

Simon wanted to get back to the happiness he had re-discovered yesterday. And so, as he waited for his connection back to Sean's house, he considered being spontaneous and jumping on a different train back to London and Catrina's bed. Yes, I'll *do* that. I'll surprise her, he thought. He felt full of devil-may-care brio.

He texted Sean as soon as he boarded the train:

Off to London again, going to surprise Catrina. She's working all day so there's a VERY good chance she won't be happy to see me. However, my plan – which I'm making up as I'm typing this! – is to wait until later this afternoon, ring her doorbell with flowers and Champagne. If she's too busy for me, fair enough, I leave the goodies, give her my best winning smile and leave. All ways round I think I'll still look like a good guy, yeah?

Sean texted back:

Good thinking, it's cool, romantic and spontaneous. The only problem, and it's not a massive problem, is that having told you she's mega-busy she might, just might, feel as if you're not taking her work seriously and it might, just might, put a dampener on the good vibes?

Simon re-read the text and agreed with his best friend.

As the return train stopped at Paddington and he climbed off he decided to go with his original plan. Just do it, he thought, the worst that can happen is she gets a bit annoyed with me, but flowers and Champagne makes a nice statement of intent and I *really* like this woman, I feel like Christian Slater in *True Romance*, although without the Elvis obsession.

He took the tube back to Camden and found a corner store near Catrina's flat. He bought the flowers and booze and walked around for a while – was it too early to knock on her door? Eventually he grew bored of hanging around. He pressed the buzzer next to her name and waited; taking a crafty look in to one of the front windows to make sure he looked his best. There was no answer, so he buzzed again. Still no answer. He decided she must be at the shops, maybe buying some milk or bread, so he would wait around for a bit. He could call or text her but that would ruin the whole romantic surprise element and *that* was the reason for being there. He began to think about waiting outside his own house on the day Meredith kept him in limbo, and when he had been confronted by the man with her in the window.

Simon was getting cold so decided to find something to do and try later. He soon reached a local cinema and waited for forty minutes to see a special screening of *Vertigo*. He had seen the film many times before and loved it – although he just couldn't bring himself to ever like Kim Novak; one of Hitchcock's iconic cool-blondes, but Simon just found her insipid.

The film ended and the house lights came up. Simon stretched and yawned. He walked outside to find the dusk settling in.

Catrina's flat wasn't far away. He bought himself a cup of coffee to heighten his senses and sipped it as he walked up to her front door again. This was a good thing he was doing, he told himself.

He looked up and saw her bedroom lights were on behind the curtains and so he buzzed her. A minute or two later the door opened. Catrina looked shocked to see him. And it registered with Simon very quickly that it was not a shocked look followed by a happy look or an annoyed look, or any look other than a *guilty* one.

'Wha ... Simon, what are you doing here? I thought we were going to text each other and stuff?' she said.

'I thought I'd bring you some things to say thanks for a lovely day yesterday. I know you're busy and I don't want to impose on your time, I just ...'

And then Simon saw a man in the hallway, a few feet behind Catrina. He was tall and lean. His face was the type that made Simon believe he enjoyed hitting people.

'Everything cool, Cat?' he said.

'Yeah, just a friend dropping some stuff,' she said. She grimaced at Simon. The man walked away.

Simon felt a tight knot of betrayal – similar to the one he had felt when Mark told him about Meredith and Dean – form in his stomach. It was a purely physical recognition that he wanted to *do* something, not always be so passive.

'What's going on? Who's *that* guy?' he said. He dropped the bag of Champagne and flowers and felt the blooming heads flop across his right foot.

Catrina breathed out and looked at her hands. 'He's another date. I met him last week. I'm sorry, Simon, I had a really nice time with you, but I think he and I fit better,' she said.

'Right. Okay. All right. That's dandy. So, er ... why did you bother meeting up with me, and then sleep with me if he's such a great fit?'

'Because I liked you and I wasn't sure about him until now.'

'I was that bad in bed? Great, thanks. So that makes *me* your Dean-option?'

'What?' Catrina said. She looked annoyed.

'What the fucky ever. Jesus, this is happening to me again, but now *I'm* the guy on the outside, the next best thing. Well, enjoy the flowers and Champagne. Enjoy the good fit guy and happy costume making. You hurricane, life-wrecking liar.'

'Sorry, Simon,' Catrina said as he walked away.

'Blah, blah, jabber, jabber,' he replied, glancing up to see the happy-hitting, good fit guy watching him from the bedroom window.

Chapter 26...

The train journey home gave Simon all the time he needed to feel *really* bad about his life, and to be as self-indulgent about his miserable luck with women as possible. He made a list of the indignity he had suffered recently, completely obscuring any part *he* had played in his own downfall. He texted his woe to Sean:

> Mudder of freaking Maoui, Catrina gimped me! She's shagging some other guy too. She met him last week; used me to compare to him, and chose him. I saw this guy and he looked like a killer. I have become DEAN! On my way back now and feeling like a complete dickhead. What a waste of time. Sorry to whine. Hopefully c u later.

Sean's reply was swift:

> That is total shit. OMG! WTF?! I guess these things happen –

unfortunately they seem to be happening to you a lot! Come on home. We'll sort things out. We'll watch the best movies available for these scenes and devise a new plan of action. Never surrender, my main man. Never.

Simon and Sean spent the evening getting drunk and watching the first two *Scream* films. By the time they switched the television off and Simon had woken from a woozy dream it had been decided that he would disengage his feelings from the blind-dating process and simply look for sex, for a while anyway. He knew, as he fell asleep, that he wasn't built for endless *casual* sex. But it would do for the time being.

Chapter 27...

The following two months were the worst of Simon's life. His boss told him he wasn't working hard enough and that the bookshop was in serious danger of closing if he couldn't come up with the requisite strategies to take on a much newer, shinier bookshop which had just opened a few minutes' walk away. Simon visited the new bookshop and took notes; he introduced himself to the manager there and asked who the best person to speak to about managerial vacancies might be.

The days at work dragged, and dragged a bit more as he spent time between legal letters regarding the house sale – he couldn't bring himself to meet with Meredith – and listening to possible *Soulmates* date voice-messages and attempting, without much conviction, to come up with an action plan to save his job.

The house sale was proceeding relatively quickly, but the pain of poring through mutual property lists and deciding who should get what seemed endless. Simon didn't want much, not the elaborately coloured sofa or the microwave or the gilt-edged mirror from over the mantlepiece in the lounge, or the Modigliani print from above their bed. Just the comfort and security of his entire old life back in hand and the ability to feel something other than a sense of perpetual motion sickness in his quest to regain an emotional life that didn't *only* include sadness about his living-state.

Sean was getting on famously with Emily. He had spent more nights away with her than with Simon recently and, even though Simon was happy for his best friend's new found love, he missed his company – texts just weren't the same; and they were taking longer to arrive. And Simon hadn't even met the woman in Sean's life yet.

Soulmates had become a compulsion for Simon; something he told himself to stop doing because it only made him feel bad. Awkward meeting after awkward meeting, judgments made fast on both sides, faces full of disappointment and the worst of the dates over in less than an hour. Simon had begun to call the date-listing: *Soulless*. But, even through the baddest of the badness, it gave him a sense of purpose; as if he was on his way somewhere. The destination was ultimate love and happiness, and he had to push on; keep going over the top into the machine gun fire one more time.

'So, tell me about the worst of the recent ones,' Sean said, referring to Simon's blind date horrors. The two friends sat in a pub near Sean's house; they had ordered fish and chips and lager.

'The three that spring to mind involve a failed ballet dancer, a lab tech who felt more for her pregnant rat than me, and a young woman who wanted telephone sex the first time we spoke and a lot more the first and last time we actually met. Trust me, I know the last one sounds great, but it wasn't. Sweet Mary, it was so

awful, the memory of it makes me want to curl into a ball and go underground.'

'Phone sex, rats and ballet? Interesting mix. I'm all ears.'

'The ballet dancer spent about an hour telling me how she had joined the English National Ballet and trained for years only to betrayed by a dancer who hated her because she got so much attention.'

'Betrayed how?' Sean asked, smiling and sipping his beer.

'Tripped, I think, ankle broken. And a new career spent teaching ballet rather than doing it. It *was* a genuinely tragic story. Trouble was, she sat there sobbing, wouldn't be consoled and left the restaurant never to return. I sat there for another forty-five minutes wondering what to do before I finally gave up on seeing her again; paid the bill and departed. I think the other diners presumed I had upset her. I got a few, *"You're a bastard"* looks as I left.'

Sean laughed and patted Simon's arm. 'Go on, tell me more, tell me more. Rats, phone sex, tell me the whole thing.'

Simon ate a mouthful of fish, took a drink and sat back.

'The lab tech used rats for medical experiments. That bit of news made me feel fairly queasy, that and the fact she had just discovered the rave scene, years after its bloody heyday of course, and the wonders of Ecstasy. So she's telling me how great rave music is, especially when you're on E, who would have guessed that, eh? And that I must get in to it as soon as possible. And then she gets a text telling her that her favourite rat is about to give birth, and so *she* leaves mid-supper, too. Although at least she left some money for the bill. She was called Mildred, the rat that is.'

Simon dipped a pair of chips in mayonnaise and ketchup and munched them, he grinned at Sean, who was trying not to laugh out loud.

'Jesus, this is priceless stuff. And okay, that's all fine and hilariously sad. But what about phone sex lady?'

Simon breathed out hard.

'How's Emily? Are you guys planning a future?' Simon said.

'Nah, nah, nah. We can talk about Emily and me later. I want to know about the phone sex nightmare.' Sean drummed his fingers on the table and then put his thumb and little finger, in the shape of a telephone receiver, to his ear.

'All right, okay. I got a message from a woman with a soft, sexy voice. It was the nicest voice I've heard since I started doing this thing. I phoned her straight back and she was on a train. We get past the whole getting to know you standard issue Q and A thing quickly, and then she started asking me about how many times I've dated using *Soulmates*. I was feeling good talking to her so I said quite a few. Suddenly she starts telling me how she loves the listings service. She loves meeting new people all the time and trying new "things".'

Simon stopped talking for a moment to pile some more fish and chips in to his mouth and wash it down with the lager, which was becoming warm.

'Finished with the food and drink? You *can't* just pause like that,' Sean said. He smiled and shook his head.

Simon nodded and ate a couple more chips. 'Before I truly registered the sway of the conversation, although obviously I felt the heat rising, she was telling me she was in the toilet and ... well, you know, doing stuff while we were talking.'

'Doing what specifically?'

'Sewing her socks mate, what do you think?'

'All right, I understand the allure of imagination. That's all good. Carry on.'

'I carried on talking, she talked some more and then we agreed to meet in London. I ...'

'Woah, Captain to-the-point. I need *more* detail than "We

talked some more". Think about Tim Roth's gangster-in-the-toilet with the sniffer-dogs anecdote in *Reservoir Dogs,* draw out the small details.'

'Well, it was the usual "What are you wearing?", "Where shall I put my hand now?" That kind of thing, until it was over.'

Sean sipped some lager, raised his eyebrows and sat back.

'The *usual* thing? You doing this kind of deal *every* day now?' he said.

Simon smiled and munched some more slightly cold cod and chips.

'Not every day, obviously. But it felt pretty natural at the time. I enjoyed the anonymity of it. It felt like part of the whole blind date thing.'

'Very *Nine and a Half Weeks.* Did she look like Kim Basinger too?'

'Hold those horses, pardner. I need to build this anecdote, as you said, the payoff will make you understand why.'

'You have my full attention, well, most of it anyway. Can I get another round in before you continue the saga?' Sean asked. He half-stood and collected the glasses.

'Absolutely.'

While Sean was at the bar Simon texted Judy:

> Hey there, Judy-Judy, how are u? Long, long time. How's Merry? And, yes, I do care about that. The house sale is almost complete, as you must know, and I just want to say that I want to stay in touch with you. I know that might cause some internal conflict, but I love you, Judy (as a friend! – I know, I'm a dick, right?) and I don't want to just lose all the years of that friendship. Anyway, enough with the rambling. Yours, Sim xxxx

Sean returned with the lagers and sat down, '*Please* carry on,' he said.

'We arranged to meet two days later, in London, in the bar of a hotel just off Leicester Square and then rang off,' Simon said. He took a swig of the lager and grinned at Sean, who looked as if he was waiting for the last and, potentially, winning number in the *National Lottery*.

'Did you ask her to text an attachment photo of herself, did you do the same?' Sean said.

'Nope. I wanted to hold on to the mystery and I guessed she did too. So I travel up to London Town and give myself enough time to arrive at the hotel and make sure I look my best. I caught the tube to Leicester Square and felt like the big winner as I climbed the escalator. The sun was out and there was a gentle breeze through the Square ...'

'Were you writing poetry?'

'What?'

'I'm dying here and you're telling me about the colour of spring! Get to the hotel, just get there and tell me what happened, pur-lease.'

'Okey doke. Christ, you are pushy, eh? You told me to draw out the details. So I arrived at the hotel and went to the loo to check teeth, hair, how red my cheeks were, that kind of thing ...'

'You checked the tone of your cheeks? Huh?'

'We *all* do shit like that, don't tell me you don't. I've seen *your* mirror face.' Simon sucked his cheeks in and made a face at Sean, who returned the look.

'And then you saw her in the bar and she looked like the sexiest vision of womanhood you've ever set your peepers on?'

'Hold up. Hang on. Yes, I saw her in the bar, but no, she wasn't ... She was the only woman in there, sitting with a vodka and tonic, looking at her watch.'

'And?'

'And I ordered a drink, introduced myself and sat down with her.'

'So mundane. What did she look like?' Sean said.

'Well that was one of the issues, the problems.'

'Issues? Did she really look *that* bad?'

'No. She had a nice face and a nice body, but ...'

'But what?'

'She ... well, truthfully, and I know this was, and is, a shitty thing to think, she looked like a cliche of a street-walking hooker.'

Simon took a drink to wet his throat, which had dried as he remembered the full extent of the humiliation he came to feel on the date.

'In specifically what way?'

'Her hair was lank and bleached blonde. Her eyes were heavy with mascara and bright pink eye-shadow, and she was wearing a mini-skirt and a ... are they called boob-tube tops? And a gold coloured bomber jacket.'

Sean winced.

'I felt like some sort of prudish old man. I also felt bad for judging her on looks, but the truth is I wasn't attracted to her *at all* and I wanted to get the hell out of there asap.'

'And, dare I ask, what happened next?'

'I think she felt uncomfortable too. My face was probably giving me away. We talked about my job briefly and then about hers. She works in a casino and she insisted on telling me how many times a night the punters try to pay her for sex. And then came the final scene, the fat lady started singing and the shit came down.'

'I'm not sure I can bear this,' Sean said. He made a face of mock-horror and sipped his drink.

Simon received a text, guessed it would be a reply from Judy; decided to read it later, and carried on with his tale.

'I asked her if she would like another drink, I thought it was only polite to stay for a while, and when she said no I started to tell her that I didn't think it would work out between us, but that it had been nice to meet her in person.'

'And?'

'And she started to shout at me. She said she had booked a room for us and asked me why I didn't want to have sex with her.'

'Oh my god. What did you say?'

'I started to waffle about chemical attraction and not wanting to dive in to a sexual thing, and she started asking me, demanding of me actually, what was so wrong with her and what made me so picky.'

'And how did you get out of that?'

'The bartender asked us to keep our voices down. And, after she had started crying, I started to be more open ...'

'Open about ... the way she looked?'

'Yep.'

'How open is *open*?'

'*Very* open. She kept asking me, kept demanding that I give her an honest explanation. So I told her about the clothes and hair thing.'

'Oh shit. And I'm going out on a guessing limb and thinking that part of the meeting wasn't the easiest?'

'Erm, no. She said she had *assumed* we would be having sex, after the phone call on the train, and couldn't get that I wasn't attracted to her in the flesh.'

'Did you actually go as far as saying that you weren't attracted to her?'

'Eventually, yes. She kept saying, over and over, "What's the matter with me then? Why don't you want to sleep with me?" I have never come across anyone like that before and I hope I never will again. It was completely surreal; as if I was part of some improv drama lesson.'

'Jesus. How did you leave things?' Sean asked. He threw back

the last of his lager and wiped his mouth.

'Well, we're not seeing each other again, that's for sure. I kept apologising and saying I hoped she'd meet someone really nice soon. And she kept telling me to fuck off. So I did. It was horrible. And I am definitely, *definitely* done with soulless *Soulmates* for a long time.'

The two friends sat and stared at each other for a few moments. Then Sean shook his head, smiled and patted Simon on the right arm.

'Bad times indeed, friend of mine. You've had a prodigiously awful run of luck. It will change soon. I know it will,' he said to Simon, who raised his eyebrows in mock-hopelessness.

'So tell me about Emily. I can't believe you've gotten so close to her and I haven't even met her yet. I guess our schedules just aren't working. When can I meet her?' Simon asked.

'Actually, I want to talk to you about that. The thing is ... the deal is... you actually *have* met her, Emily, that is. She isn't the guitar girl either, that ended before it began, sort of,' Sean said.

'What? I've met Emily? Where? In the bookshop?'

'No, not in the shop, although I guess she might have visited you there at some point.'

'Visited me? What are you on about?'

'Okay, all right. This is a tough one to detail, so I'm just gonna say it ... Emily is *Judy* and we're getting married soon.' Sean sat back and looked at his hands and then, slowly, he looked up at Simon – whose face had become fixed in an expressionless gaze at the table between them. 'Simon? You all right?' Sean said.

Simon couldn't think of anything for a moment or two, or three. And then he thought of his friend and his feelings.

'Yeah, I mean fucky duck doo-da. *Judy*. I thought she hated your ass. I thought you hated hers too. How? When? Tell me the whole thing. And why call her Emily?'

Sean pretended a sly look and tapped his nose.

'Think about Judy's middle name ... Emily, right? We didn't want to rub the romance in your face. It's been such a shit period for you and Merry.'

Simon sat up straight. 'Does Merry know about the two of you?' he said.

'By accident, yeah. She came back early from work one afternoon.'

'How did it start? I mean, after that time you two went out and things turned real sour I assumed you wouldn't share space in a building, let alone a bed.'

'You and me, and Judy, both ... all. It started up again when she came to see me, at work, to talk about Merry's new guy who, by the by, she dumped recently.'

Simon shrugged in reply to the news about his ex, but felt something inside – something like hope and excitement – at the thought that she was single again, like him.

'Anyhow, Judy was so upset, and I hadn't seen her so ... open and emotional before. Odd though it sounds, especially from a notorious git like me, I was moved by it, by her. It was impossible to talk at work, so I suggested we meet afterwards and talk more.'

'Can I get a couple more drinks in before you carry on?' Simon said. Sean nodded; looking a bit surprised at the sudden stop.

Simon went to the bar, ordered two more lagers – considered ordering whiskey shots too but changed his mind. As he waited he checked the message on his mobile. It was a reply from Judy:

> Hi Simon, that was a lovely text (and don't worry, I feel safe knowing you'll always be a dick!) Merry's fine, doing well. And yes, we must, and will, stay in touch. Hope you're having a nice evening. Love, Judy xxx

Simon smiled. Three kisses – she was in love with his

best friend! He wanted to fire back a reply, along the lines of: Hey Emily, or is it still Judy? I know what *you* did last summer ... xxx (That's **three** kisses, the last one is from your lover-boy here with me!) But he decided doing something like that would be unfunny and offensive, and he had Sean's feelings to think of now.

Simon paid for and collected the drinks and turned around to see Sean finish a text – he knew it would be sent to Judy. She would know that he knew now.

'Okay. Let's go on,' Simon said, passing Sean his glass.

Sean took a sip and put the glass down. 'So we met up and talked for two, maybe three, hours. And by the time we parted it was obvious there was a lot of ... chemical attraction there.'

'Oh, thanks for the reminder about sodding chemical attractions,' Simon said. He grinned at Sean, who winked.

'Seriously though, I couldn't stop thinking about her. I texted her that evening and we met up a day or two later, and then it went mad. We talked and texted all day every day. We saw each other as much as we could and it's been amazing. *She's* amazing. And, well, two days ago I asked her to marry me and she said yes.'

'That's just the most ... good for you, Sean. I am so happy for you, mate. It *is* amazing. When are you getting hitched? Married I mean, hitched sounds so grubby.'

'Two weeks time. We've booked the registry office; got a place sorted for a lunch and invited some other folks. I'd like you to be my best man. I will understand if it's just too weird though.'

'It *is* a bit weird, but I wouldn't miss it for the world. Of course. Thank you. It would be a true honour,' Simon said, and he meant it – happiness at last for his best friend and made from the ashes of his relationship. There was some good to be found. And then it occurred to Simon that the marriage would mean he only had a short time left living in Sean's house.

'I'll talk to my parents and move in with them as soon as I can,' he said.

'No hurry mate. We're going to honeymoon in the Seychelles for a fortnight. That gives you a month minimum, yeah?'

'Great, thanks. Although, with the money from the house sale I should be looking to get my own place. It's just really hard to think of starting over again without Merry ... anyway, sorry, I don't want to rain on your parade. This is such fantastic news.'

Chapter 28...

Two weeks went by with Simon trying to avoid Sean. He didn't want to show his friend how nervous he felt about the wedding – no groom needed to see his Best Man wigging out. But Simon felt full of anxiety. He even began to ask himself what The Saint might do if this was an episode of the television series. But that didn't help at all, because Simon knew the TV hero would have jumped in his sports car and driven off to Monaco rather than face mundane realities like this.

Simon's stress wasn't just the usual mix of nerves because of having to make a speech and not let his best friend down at a crucial time; but also the deep core of insecurity whenever he thought about seeing Meredith again. He felt guilty for the way their life together had imploded – almost to the point where he had forgotten what precipitated the split.

There were likely to be around fifty guests at the registry office and then the reception – not quite enough to avoid Meredith completely. And, in the moments of night-time honesty, when the lights were out and Simon lay alone in the quiet, he knew he didn't

want to avoid her any longer. He wanted to see her and talk to her, watch her smile again. It felt like decades since he had seen her smile.

He bought a new suit, shirt and tie and brushed his shoes shiny clean the night before the wedding. And then found he couldn't sleep at all. So he got up, drinking red wine at four in the morning – Sean was sleeping over at his parents' house – and watched John Cusack fall in love with Kate Beckinsale in *Serendipity*.

The alarm on his mobile phone woke him at seven; his head felt heavy and he thought he might vomit. He made some bagels and coffee, and after forcing down his breakfast he cold-showered and dressed. He was meeting Sean at nine to go through the plans for the day one last time.

He sent Sean a text to make sure he was up and all right:

Mate, u ok? Still up for nine o'clock? Couldn't sleep last night; ended up watching Johnny Cusack woo Kate Beckinsale in Serendipity. Not a bad film, bit formulaic, I thought. Hard to believe it was directed by the same guy who made Hear My Song, eh? Anyways, hope u're ok. C u shortly. S

Sean replied:

Doing ok. Had a hearty breakfast. Mum and dad insisting on treating this like Xmas morning; had me up and eating at six-thirty. Nice though. Am defo up for nine chat still. Lkg 4wd to c-ing u. Hope u're ok too. Ciao for now.

Simon smiled and deleted the message. He felt *far* from okay, but wanted to suck in his nerves and just *be there* for Sean – return so many favours to his best friend.

The two friends arrived at the registry office just under an hour before the ceremony. They waited inside on a bench; they were the first to arrive.

'You all right?' Simon asked Sean, who had hardly said a word in fifteen minutes; completely out-of-character.

'Bricking it, but okay. I guess it's all natural and good to be scared shitless, yeah?' Sean replied.

'Perfectly normal, natural, yeah.'

'I can't quite believe I'm getting married, and I don't mean to Judy, just *married*. It's all happened so fast. But it feels so right as well, you know?'

'I do. I was there, or almost there once, too.'

'Yeah, that's true. You going to be all right seeing Merry again?'

'Yeah, absolutely. It'll be strange at first, but the day is about you and Judy and that's all that matters to me,' Simon said. Sean turned and smiled at him. They hugged and patted each other on the back.

And then Simon saw Judy and Meredith coming through the double entrance doors. Judy's parents followed behind them, and then a number of semi-familiar faces began to stream in. Simon nodded at Sean; then towards the door. Sean shot up and walked over to greet his future wife and the various guests. Simon did the same. He smiled at Judy, who grinned back – she looked full of happiness and Simon's anxiety began to drift away. Then he turned to Meredith, who was looking in the opposite direction.

'Hi, Merry. How are you?' he said.

'I'm all right. How are you, Sim?' she said. She seemed uncomfortable and didn't make direct eye contact, but Simon was just happy to be near her.

'I'm good, thanks. It's lovely to see you again. You look very beautiful.'

'Thanks. You look very hand ... smart, too.'

Before Simon could attempt any more of his "magic" chat on Meredith he noticed the registrar waving at him. It was time for Sean and Judy to get married.

'I'd love to talk to you later, Merry. I think we've got to get them in now ... Sean and Judy, that is. The registrar's waiting.'

'Sure. Let's talk later,' she said. And then she smiled at him, and Simon thought he might fall to his knees. The smile was worth at least ten kisses on the end of any text – a *real* smile, not a: "*You've fucked up my life, but this is a big day for our best friends and I have to smile at your stupid face*"smile.

He still loved her, and maybe, if he was really lucky – regardless of the recent lack of luck-evidence derived from his *Soulmates* encounters – she might still love him.

Chapter 29...

Simon's speech got the right number of laughs for him to feel as if he had done a good job. There were a couple of moments when only Sean and Judy had laughed, but that was all right too; it was *their* day. He had stayed away from too many film references, drawn a complete line through any ex-girlfriend anecdotes and been emotionally honest about how he felt about his two friends getting married.

'I can truthfully say that I can't think of any two people I would rather see together. Please raise your glasses for the bride and groom,' he said, holding his Champagne aloft. The guests joined him. He looked down at Sean, who was kissing Judy, and then he looked at Meredith, who was smiling at him. But she looked sad, as if he had given something precious away and excluded her. And then he wondered if she was upset about his slightly cavalier – albeit in-keeping with the occasion – comment just before: '... can't think of any two people I would rather see together.'

There was music and dancing – Simon found himself feeling tipsy from the Champagne and even more light-headed from sucking in helium from the many balloons attached to each flower arrangement in the middle of the tables. He frugged around the dancefloor in approximations of dance moves, and joined Judy and Sean in throwing shapes to Soft Cell's version of *Tainted Love* – Judy's favourite song. And even though Simon was enjoying himself, he couldn't help but continuously glance around the room to re-locate Meredith; he wanted to make sure she was near for the moment when he finally had enough adrenalin in his system to talk to her.

'Mate, that was a great speech, thanks for keeping it clean and simple,' Sean said. He hugged Simon. 'How's it going with Merry? You *seem* to be coping well.'

'It's freaking weird, out of reality weird actually. But also okay. Strange, eh? I feel as if this day is part of life before the Dean thing happened; as if I'm being given a second go-around,' Simon said and smiled.

'She looks a bit down. Have you spoken about ... stuff yet?'

'I'm going to do that right here and right now. I've already waited too long. Sean, I know this is your day and I really don't want to do or say anything to ruin any part of that. I just want to say thank you for looking after me, after the thing happened with Merry. You are the best friend a guy could have. You protected me and helped me carry on through all that crap. I won't ever be able to thank you enough. But I can make a start. Thank you.'

They hugged again. And Simon carried on, 'I hope you won't be too disappointed about this next bit. You advised me a while ago to move forward and risk starting over when Merry and I first split up. But the thing is, I love her, I love her with all my heart and soul. I can't live without her, as painful a cliché as that is. I hope you won't think I'm a big prat if I try and win her back?'

Sean breathed out and raised his eyebrows.

'I didn't see *that* coming.' He smiled. 'Actually, I *did* kind of see it coming. I know you still love her. And no one can say you haven't tried to move forward. Listen, it's your life, you have to follow your heart ... jeez, I'm wheeling them out now, eh? But seriously, being with Judy again and getting married has changed the way I think about the patterns of life. If I can get to this point, you can too, and you should try. Not everything *has* to be fubar. Do it today, now.'

Sean patted Simon on the shoulder and walked off to see his new wife.

Simon looked through a grouping of guests to see Meredith sitting alone, holding a glass of Champagne and writing a text. He wondered for a moment if the text was being composed for Dean, or some other Dean-type in her life – but he dismissed the thought and berated himself for the onset of cynicism. Today *had* to be about beginnings. He walked across the room and pulled a chair to sit next to her.

'Hello there,' he said.

She looked up, seeming initially startled.

'Oh, hi, Sim. Good speech. You okay, having a nice time?'

'Yes. Yes I am. I was wondering if we could talk?'

'Sure. Here?'

'Here is good. Do you mind if I say what's on my mind, just get it out there?'

'As long as it's not a recrimination filled rant, then yes, okay.' Meredith smiled at Simon – that smile, that *real* smile for him again.

'No more recriminations. The thing is ... well, I don't know about you but I always felt like the end of *When Harry met Sally* was a bit of a cop-out, a bit of a way of satisfying the US marketplace, the whole New Year's party thing, romance and happy endings. Do you know what I mean?'

Meredith laughed and shook her head knowingly. 'You and Sean have been spending *way* too much time together,' she said.

Simon laughed. 'That may be true, but the reason I mention the film and the ending when they finally get together is because ... well, because I've been thinking about you so much leading up to today, wondering if you're happy, okay in life and how ... whether or not you miss me, us, the house, all the rest of that stuff.'

Meredith looked at her hands, she turned them over and back – a gesture Simon knew from old; she was nervous.

'Of course I miss you and the way things were, but we can't just pretend things are fine now. What about the thing with Dean? And anyway the house is gone,' she said.

'Dean is the *past*. And I don't want to ever live in the past again. And true, things have been awful, the worst. But this time apart has taught me that we're *all* fools, that we all overreach and fail, and that judging the person you love when they're reaching out and asking for the ultimate thing ... love and forgiveness ... is about the worst thing you can do. Oh fuck, I'm not saying any of this right. Meredith ...' Simon reached out and took her left hand, expecting her to pull it away, but she didn't. '... I love you beyond comparison. I've tried to live without you and I don't want to do that anymore. *You* are my life. To be really corny about it and misquote Harry at the close of the film, "And it's not because I'm lonely, and it's not because it's a wedding. I came here today because when you realise you want to spend the rest of your life with somebody, you want the rest of your life to start as soon as possible."

'Does that mean you're *over* what happened? I can't undo what I did. I am so sorry about all of that. It's just that without trust we couldn't really begin to ...' she said.

'As I said it's in the past, dead and buried. I only want to think about the future, about us. Can *you* forgive *me* for not trying harder, and being such a self-absorbed fool?'

'This is beginning to feel like a Richard Curtis film scene,' Meredith said. She squeezed and rubbed Simon's hand.

'Hopefully more *Four Weddings and a Funeral* than *The Boat that Rocked*,' Simon said. They both laughed.

And then they didn't speak again for a while. Meredith held his hand, rubbing it and squeezing it over and over – as if he might disappear. She smiled at him, tears in her eyes. He smiled back, not thinking of anything but her. But two songs came in to Simon's mind – one great and one cheesy: *Sound of Silence* and *When You Say Nothing At All*.

And he realised that sometimes you *really* don't need to say a word.

Daniel Gothard lives in Oxford with his wife and three children. He has a CertHE and MA in creative writing. He has previously had two novels published and appeared in numerous literary journals and anthologies in the UK and abroad. His last novel – *Friendship and Afterwards* – was nominated for The People's Book Prize. He is also an Arts Correspondent for After Nyne magazine.

REMEMBER TO BREATHE

by

Simon Pont

£7.99

ISBN 9781909273009

REMEMBER TO BREATHE
SIMON PONT

Remember that time when Twitter sounded like an insult, no one had a Facebook page, and Britney Spears still looked innocent in pig tails?

Remember to Breathe is a rom-com trip set to a retro beat, for anyone who's ever partied like it was 1999. And woken to realise that the last tequila was very unwise. Samuel Grant seems to have it all – a brilliant job, a beautiful girlfriend, and fabulous hair. But even those who have it all can throw it all away when they have too much of a good thing...

Remember to Breathe invites you to enjoy the highs and lowly lows of Samuel's life as he ushers in the new century in his own inimitable style. Join Samuel as he dances to the rhythm of London's pulse, and often finds he dances with two left feet.

Available in paperback and ebook at Amazon and
http://urbanepublications.com/books/remember-to-breathe/

CLOSE OF PLAY

by

P.J. Whiteley

£7.99

ISBN 9781909273528

Brian Clarke has an ordered life, a life of village cricket, solid principles, and careful interaction with those around him. He is resolutely fending off advancing middle-age with a straight bat, determined to defend his wicket against life's occasional fast balls. Then he meets Elizabeth – a gentle, caring, genuinely selfless soul who is a glowing bloom amongst the ordered hedgerows of his existence. As Elizabeth demands Brian's interest...and breathes hope into his heart...he must reassess his self-defined role as the lone batsmen and fight to find the courage to fall in love. Or risk losing her forever.

Close of Play is a thoughtful, funny, beautifully honest story of love and manners. It's a tale of missed opportunities and a chance at redemption – and the fear of opening our hearts to another when we think we've forgotten how to love.

Available in paperback and ebook at Amazon and http://urbanepublications.com/books/close-of-play/

URBANE